DOLL CRIMES

KAREN RUNGE

Let the world know:
#IGotMyCLPBook!

Crystal Lake Publishing
www.CrystalLakePub.com

Be sure to sign up for our newsletter and receive
a free eBook: http://eepurl.com/xfuKP

ISBN: 978-1-64669-314-6

Editor:
Monique Snyman—http://www.moniquesnyman.com

Layout:
Lori Michelle—www.theauthorsalley.com

Cover Art:
Ben Baldwin—www.benbaldwin.co.uk

Proofread by:
Paula Limbaugh
Gwendolyn Nix

WELCOME TO
CRYSTAL LAKE
PUBLISHING

TALES FROM THE
DARKEST DEPTHS

Welcome to another
Crystal Lake Publishing creation.

Thank you for supporting independent publishing and small presses. You rock, and hopefully you'll quickly realize why we've become one of the world's leading publishers of Dark and Speculative Fiction. We have some of the world's best fans for a reason, and hopefully we'll be able to add you to that list really soon. Be sure to sign up for our newsletter to receive some free eBooks, as well as info on new releases, special offers, and so much more.

**Welcome to Crystal Lake Publishing—
Tales from the Darkest Depths.**

OTHER TITLES BY KAREN RUNGE

Seven Sins: Stories (Concord Free Press)
Seeing Double (Grey Matter Press)

OTHER NOVELS BY CRYSTAL LAKE PUBLISHING

The Mourner's Cradle: A Widow's Journey by Tommy B. Smith
House of Sighs (with sequel novella) by Aaron Dries
Aletheia: A Supernatural Thriller by J.S. Breukelaar
Where the Dead Go to Die by Mark Allan Gunnells
and Aaron Dries
Blackwater Val by William Gorman
Pretty Little Dead Girls: A Novel of Murder and Whimsy
by Mercedes M. Yardley

For Erika

Mother is the name for God in the lips and hearts of little children.
—William Makepeace Thackeray, 'Paradise Lost'

I talk in a daze, I walk in a maze
I cannot get out, said the starling.
—Vladimir Nabokov, 'Lolita'

1

MY MOTHER, SHE'S standing at the counter with her hair shining loose over her shoulder, her eyes just as bright, her smile so wide she can only be oblivious to the lipstick marks on her teeth. She's laying her change out onto the counter, one coin at a time, placing each down with a sharp, metallic *tap* on the smooth space between the till and the gum rack. The tapping sound, clear and deliberate behind the dancing wall of her voice, feels like the echo of a giant clock in the background. Ticking down to something. *Tap-tap* like *tick-tock*.

"Eighty-nine," she says. *Tap-Tick*. "Ninety." *Tap-Tock*.

Beside the rows of coins, stacked up to tens in neat piles, are two crisp bills. Beside the bills are her intended purchases. There are only three—a vanilla-scented lip balm, a box of salted crackers, and a carton of full-cream milk.

"One hundred," she beams. *Tap. Tick.* "Nearly there."

She's twenty cents off the total. She's fumbling in the depths of her bag in search of more loose change. The guy behind the counter, he's standing there with his arms folded, trying to look serious while he stares down her shirt. She's made this easy for him—the staring—leaning forward the way she is, her shoulders curved in the way they are.

The man waiting behind my mom, he huffs a sigh. It

comes out mostly through his nose. His hands tighten on his shopping basket. He wants to buy a frozen pizza, a bottle of soda water, a tube of lubricant. Clearly, he's not asking much of life as it is, and this is supposed to be the express queue.

My mother looks over her shoulder at him. Maybe she caught the gust on the back of her neck, felt his breath hit the space between her shoulders. "Sorry," she says to him. "I'm in a hurry, too." She gives him the kind of smile that leaves him awkward for a few moments. His cheeks color to a tough, meaty red. He huffs again. But this time it isn't a sigh. Not exactly.

"I'll pay whatever's left," the woman behind Lube Dude says. She's middle-aged, no makeup, sloppy ponytail and sports shoes that have never seen the surface of any track or indoor court. She wants to buy a pack of tampons, a bottle of aspirin, a box of cheese-flavored crackers, and the obligatory bread, eggs, and milk, of course. Still, it isn't hard to tell why she's testy.

"Five," my mother says, ignoring her. "Six."

Tick. And then *Tock.*

The shop is small but understaffed. Four check-outs, two in use. The guy behind the counter should've done something by now, but he's young, new. Who expects this kind of scene on a calm, mid-week afternoon?

He clears his throat. "Ma'am . . . ."

My mother stops counting. "Yes?"

"Don't worry about the rest," he says. "Please."

So, at fourteen cents short, everyone in line behind my mother exhales a loud sigh of relief.

"But . . . are you sure?" she opens her eyes wide at him, and smiles again, the tips of her teeth caught with the scarlet smudge of her lipstick. Red smeared on white. Gleaming.

"Yes, really," the cashier guy says. "It doesn't matter. Just, please . . . "

2

His new worry is she's going to launch into a thank you speech. That she'll stay right where she is with her shining hair and her stained smile, and hold the queue up even longer while she tells him how *wonderful* he is, how *kind* he is, how he can only be an *angel*, helping a stranger out so selflessly. From the way she's standing—cozy on her elbows, her feet arched in their heels with one ankle crossed back in a lazy twist—this seems a likely scenario. The way she leans, it's like she's at her own kitchen counter. The way she's smiling, it's like she's catching up with an old friend.

"Please," he says.

My mother seems unsure. She turns her head for a moment, about to look back again at the growing line of people—now six, maybe seven—behind her, but thinks better of it and returns her attention to the cashier. He drags his eyes away from the place on her chest where her shirt ends and her skin starts. For a moment he looks like he might be about to cry.

"Well, times are tough for all of us," my mother says.

Cashier Man stares at her. He blinks.

"So . . . I can't tell you how grateful I am. My little girl here—" and now she points to me "—she and I, we struggle every damn day to support ourselves and each other. Every cent counts. Every cent *really* counts. So few folks understand that when it's not them it's happening to. You know?"

The cashier guy definitely knows. Minimum wage for long shifts, school assignments, and debt payments. Time stretched out like a decaying rubber band you have to keep plucking on, dreading the day when it finally snaps—but then he has a moment. He seems to replay what he's heard, and he looks at me. Eyes mostly white.

"That's your *daughter*?"

My mother beams. "Looks just like me, doesn't she?"

My mother, sometimes she's a super bitch.

"Hey." I smile. My teeth are whiter than my mother's. They don't have any lipstick marks. "Mind if I take some gum?"

I've already pocketed a pack, strawberry-flavored, by the time he looks at me.

"S-sure," he says.

I take another pack. The only one he knows about.

"It's so important to be *kind* in this life," my mother says.

"I thought maybe she was your sister," Cashier Dude mumbles. He's trying not to look at me again.

My mother scoops the cash back up off the counter. Bills, coins, the lot. She shoves it all into the pocket of her leather jacket. She picks up the purchases. The items she hasn't purchased at all.

"Only great people do beautiful things," she says. She cocks an eye at me, signalling that it's time to leave.

"But—" the cashier says. "Wait—"

But.

Wait.

Like by the time he dared to say those words, they still had any power at all.

My mother zips up the side pocket of her jacket, packed now with all the cash she's just re-appropriated. She shoves the milk carton into my hands. She palms the lip balm in his full view.

"God bless you," she says. "*So* much."

I follow her out, and when the door closes behind me I hear a bell jingle inside.

Such a cheerful sound.

The stiff silence of sudden outrage shut behind.

***

"Okay kitten," my mother says as we speed-walk across the parking lot. "Stay right by me for the next few blocks, okay?"

4

I wouldn't know where else to go, but this is something she always says after what she calls a 'paper-tiger heist'. The famous paper tiger, a cut-out form that fools only the utterly gullible or the absolutely stupid. My mother, she's not made of paper, though. The tiger in her has teeth. Scarlet-marked and all.

That we've just risked a major scene for some milk and crackers, it's not important. Adrenalin, endorphins, the sweet mayhem-jolt anxiety and excitement make when they swirl into each other. My heart pounds. My throat is swollen with all the giggles I'm keeping trapped down there. Scary as it is right now, it's also sort of funny. Later it'll be hilarious.

"Try to look *innocent*," she tells me over her shoulder, half-smile, fast-stepping in her heels. I've never seen any other woman walk so fast with spikes on her feet. Battered concrete or rough country road, my mother steps like all the world is her linoleum.

The box of crackers slides out from under the clasp of her jacket—it thuds against the concrete and rolls onto a battered side. Probably all shattered in there, now.

"Goddammit," she mumbles, pausing to snatch the box up, glancing at me through the fall of her hair.

I raise an eye at her, flash her the tube of lubricant, the carton of eggs. I lifted them right out of those tight-clenched baskets while their holders gazed in stunned outrage at my mother's shining-smile antics. I could've swirled these items over my head on the way out, shrieking, and nobody would've noticed. Back there, I was that invisible and she was that bright.

"My girl." She grins.

Without having to try this time, I smile.

I don't know where we're going, but she leads us. My momma in her pretty spiked shoes, with her lovely dark lips.

Her blonde hair glittering, her silhouette stark as black velvet tossed on tall flames. Like an angel on fire. Like a shadow thrown against the sun.

2

MY MOM WAS fifteen years old when I arrived in her world, and the way she tells it, you'd swear there was never a sign for her that she was even pregnant.

"You gave me the worst cramps I ever had in my life," she's said to me. Like I was a forgotten tampon or a plate of bad seafood. "But when I first saw you, it made it all okay."

I know it's not *okay*, and she knows it's not *okay*, but since so much of life is pretending what's horribly wrong is actually *really okay*, maybe the truth doesn't matter so much in the end.

Pretend okay. Real okay. Maybe there isn't always a difference. A teenager gets pregnant, or not. A baby is born, or not. So many beautiful, terrible journeys leading out from so many different possibilities. Like a pane of glass cracking, fractures making fractures, a fragile crisscross of lines spreading out in a spiderweb shatter.

"When something scary happens, or something hurts you, you have to weigh the bad up against the good it gives," she says. "You have to trust when you look back on it one day, you'll see all the ways it was pretty. You have to look for the beauty, babe. It's always there."

I don't remember where we were when we last had this conversation, but I see a lollipop in her mouth. I see her squint-smile, the one where her eyes get tiny and the dimples in her cheeks scoop hollows into her face. She presses the lollipop to her lower lip. Wet, electric red. It vanishes back into her mouth. A small red orb holding down her tongue.

What she doesn't say. What I always think. Even if you do find a lot of good from something bad, nothing really makes it all the way *okay*. Scars, bruises, fears. They still happened. They're still there. This is the truth nobody likes to look at, while they're dewy-eyed talking about how *grateful* they are for some vicious event that damn-near destroyed them.

Bad things turn the good life that follows into a consolation prize. I guess this is what I am to her. Her consolation prize.

My mother doesn't talk much about before I was born. She says as she is now, she can't imagine being without me. She says this like nothing that came before me exists for her anymore. Like I wiped it out, shredded it into a fine mist. Those memories are wisps and ghosts hovering around her, half-complete. Not solid enough to take seriously.

"I didn't have a reason for living before you," she's told me.

And.

"Becoming a mother is like dying in a car wreck and coming back a different person."

And.

"Not all types of dying are bad."

The part of her life before me, I don't think any of it was particularly fair or easy. Not *real okay*, not *pretend okay* either.

"You don't have to be what you grew up around," she says. "But that doesn't mean it's not a part of you."

I don't remember where we were going when we had this conversation, but I see her behind the wheel of a car, driving us somewhere. The visors are down. Her sunglasses mask her eyes. The sun is bright and low against the horizon. Her forehead shines with sweat.

"It was just a small town, doll. One of a million. Nothing special about it. *Believe* me."

She's described it for me, though—the town and the hills surrounding it—a little place lost in the middle of rural nowhere, surrounded by woods and rocks, gathering up towards the mountains in thickening waves.

"They scared me as a kid," she says. "Not the woods, but the mountains further out. Some of those mountains are shaped like tables. Big and wide and flat at the top, you know? I used to think giants lived out in the hills somewhere. I used to have nightmares about them coming at night and snatching people out of their beds. Using the mountains like furniture, sitting down at one of them like it was a dinner table. Laying their victims out, all tiny and screaming, all wriggling around on the plate. Sometimes in my dreams the giants even had cutlery—massive knives and forks that flashed silver and made sounds like thunder when they moved."

I don't think the giants lived in the hills. I think the giants *were* the hills. Mossy faces and broken teeth. A turned shoulder here, a bent knee there, making all those shapes.

"Yeah, it was full of monsters, all right," Momma says.

I don't remember where we were here either, but I see us sitting on the curve of a road at night. A hill stumbles down below us in a sheer and shadowed fall, soft with wild grass. Streetlights shine above and behind, picking up the diamond sequins on her denim jacket when she moves. I feel myself shivering in my skin. Shivering from the cold, or maybe for her.

"That man," she says—her father, who she never calls *father*, who I'd never call *grandfather*—"He didn't have a lot to give. Even if he did, he didn't do a lot of giving."

I guess she was poor or maybe it means he was selfish. My momma, she never talks about those details. She barely mentions her own mother at all.

"I don't remember her, babe," she says when I ask, tossing her hair over her shoulder so the streetlights ripple-shine through it. "So take a good look at *me*, huh? You should be so lucky." Nudging me. "You got a mother and a best friend all in one, and I'm right here next to you." Laughing. "Drink me in." Looping her arm through mine. The diamonds on her shoulders flash again. Pressing a kiss to the side of my face. Her breath warm and sweet.

The way she talks about it, I imagine my mom's room was all bare walls and a baseboard bed. She doesn't have to describe it in exact words. The truths words make can be different to how a thing actually is. Dark places make dark pictures, and sometimes I think I see every corner.

The baseboard for her bed, the way I picture it, it was the splintery kind. She slept hard, when she slept. It toughened her skin, but not in a way you know by looking or touching. The curtains were smoke-stained, hanging from broken hooks so the light splashed down on her even when they were shut. I see a stash of sweets and a coil of junk necklaces she's saved, hidden somewhere smart—a false floorboard or a hollow behind a loose section of skirting board. She's good at hiding things, which is a talent more than a learned skill.

"I was a grownup way before I was supposed to be. Before I even knew it was supposed to be any different for kids," she says. "But hey. People with easy childhoods grow up to be a bunch of clueless brats. You ever notice that?"

I don't know.

Maybe.

My mom, there's a lot of things she notices. Since she had to grow up with nobody looking after her but herself, she's sharper than most other people in a lot of ways. When I was younger, I thought there was nothing she didn't know how to do. She can change a tire, jump-start a car, sew a button, roll a cigarette, make a meal out of near-nothing, put lipstick on without a mirror, and tie a cherry stalk with her tongue.

"It's okay to ask for help the first time," she says. "But then you pay attention. You watch. You remember. Then you'll never have to ask again."

If I think of her hometown, I imagine railway tracks for some reason, but this can't be a real memory. Not of mine. It just feels that way—like metal and dust and iron lines slicing through soft earth. I think of That Man and her, together in his house, and then of me, a bud blooming in her belly. Me, rounding out so fast and tight she couldn't push me flat with bandages, couldn't smother me with loose fabric. Like I was a tumor, or maybe more like an earthquake rippling up against her surface, making new shapes under her skin. The damage getting harder for her to hide.

Slut. She says that man called her that when those oversized sport shirts and lumpy sweaters couldn't hide me anymore.

Whore. He said that, too.

Fifteen years old, sobbing in her bedroom. I see her flat on her belly, her hair flung out onto her pillows. Or, no. She can't have been flat on her belly, not with me in there. But I'm sure about the hair? Tangled, dirty. Darker than it is now.

"I was still myself," she tells me. "I was still the same girl, only pregnant. But to everyone I'd ever known, I was now stained. Overnight, I was trash. People can be fucking awful when something they don't like happens to you. Something they wouldn't like happening to them, or to their family. You're the one in front of them, so you're the one they blame. Like demonizing you gives them some kind of protection. Next thing, you've got nobody close and nowhere to go. Know what I mean?"

I do know. Sort of. I don't know. Not really. Especially since this is as much as she'll say about the other people in this story. Nothing at all about my father, not a word about his own reaction to the news. Or if he was even still around.

Slut.

Whore.

The man who gave me half his genes, she's never once said his name, which makes me wonder if she knows herself. Who was he? It's like she has a list of possibilities, but none of them fit the idea in her head. So she'd rather say he's *Nobody.* Like I was her own creation, her own conjuring. In a lot of ways, I guess I am.

"I grew up different too," she says. "Worlds from that whole *nuclear family* bullshit. But even the way I grew up, I never had someone the way you have me. I wasn't so lucky, babe."

Her childhood home was a kind of chaos factory. A constant stream of people coming and going. Neighbors, strangers. Her father's friends. His acquaintances. The back room kept dark, the windows opened to cracks behind heavy black curtains.

"It wasn't a place for children," she's said.

The first time my mother got drunk, she was only about eight or nine.

"Some old dude kept giving me sips of his whiskey," she smiles. Her bitter smile, when a memory is almost good but has a lot of bad around it too.

This conversation? I think we were at a bus depot, waiting to leave. Sitting on our bags outside the ticket office. Dawn was dragging night into day. The air was so fresh and so chill even our breaths were mist. We were huddled back against the cold brick wall with our arms locked around our legs. We'd taken some clothes out of our bags to lay over ourselves for extra warmth. The sky was a crisp ghost-blue, like when the day is warming up hot after a night full of ice.

"I remember feeling kinda giddy, like I'd been spinning around and my head hadn't stopped swirling yet. I was happy—woozy-happy. I was stumbling all over the place. Bumping into everything. It can't have been, you know. *Safe*."

"No one helped you?" I said.

"*Helped* me? No babe. That Man and his *friends*, they thought it was funny. They all stood around and laughed at me. They gave me more. They gave me so much I threw up behind the television set. Then I got so scared of being punished for it that I peed, right there on the carpet. 'This little thing hasn't been house-trained yet', one guy said. I remember, because I remember thinking *'Thing'*? And how awful that word felt, the way he was saying it. I was just a kid, drunk and confused and crying, with pee running down my legs and puke burning the back of my tongue, while they stood around and looked down at me, laughing."

I see these strangers, looming over her. Big men with hands spaced wide on their hips, heads thrown back. I see her wide eyes and her soiled dress, the tip of her tongue between her teeth the way she does when she's scared. I see her weaving on her feet.

The way my momma tells her bad memories, they always sound worse than mine.

I don't know why there were so many people at her house—there always are, in all her stories—or what exactly *That Man* did for a living. I want to imagine a poker lounge, a kind of backyard gambling den. I've been in one or two before, so I know how they look. Cards and cigarette smoke and crumpled stacks of cash. Empty beer bottles cluttering the tables, lined up against the walls. Everything smelling sour like ash and days-old sweat. Unwashed hair and dirty shirts. It's easy to see my mother in this place.

"That Man was useless," my mother tells me. "*Useless*. He barely did anything except open and close the door to let those bozos in and out. And drink. And talk. Always, lots of talk. Like he was this incredible human being who knew everything better than anyone, though he hardly left the house. Mostly though, I guess he was just lazy. I once heard a woman talking about That Man, back when I was a little kid, younger than you are now. She was telling someone, 'If there was work in the bedroom, he'd want to take a nap.' The way she said it, I knew it was supposed to be funny, but it was years before I understood what it meant."

My mother didn't laugh when she first heard this saying, but I did when she first told it to me.

I guess, unlike her, I was old enough to get the joke.

3

WHERE WE ARE now, this town has been *home* for a touch over two weeks. It's a moderate size suburban square, sprawling, kinda poor but not trash-torn. There's a water tower up on one of the higher hills, which you can see from almost everywhere around. It doesn't look so big from a distance, though it must be, or it wouldn't loom like that. Metal bars and splayed legs. A dome-topped cage held high. The high street isn't long but it snakes around in sections, hiding the post office behind the supermarket, the library behind the mechanics. I don't know where the schools are yet—maybe tucked farther back.

My mother says this town is a perfect 'launch pad'. Small, safe. Separate, but connected. It has a coach depot and a train line and a highway running by. It's a place with many exits. No locked doors. We live like rumors in towns like this. Sketch-book versions of ourselves with scratched-out features and unknown names. Vague address, no kin. This is the kind of town we get to stay in long enough to find a rhythm, feel familiar. Settle down on shallow roots. The type of weed that tears out with one easy tug, and barely turns the soil. Some towns like this, we get close to forgetting we're not really supposed to stay. Staying too long makes leaving difficult, like the way leaving Auntie Clem was difficult.

Our friend here's name is Susie. I want to tell him he's got a girl's name, but I don't know if that would be safe. How he would react. His eyes are soft when he looks at me, but I've seen him clenching his hands when he's stressed, pushed, unsure. They open and shut in slow-grasp spasms, like he's looking for something lost in the air around his hips.

Hey, Little Kitten, he calls me. *Darling. Pretty One. Doll.*

He says these names smirking like a friend, like a joke, hands on his hips, his shoulder shrugging like, *Shucks*. There's nothing sharp in his eyes, and the way he says it makes me giggle, or at least smile. That smirk of his, it's the safe type. So far.

"You could be your mom's sister," he said the day we first met. "Her baby half-sister. Same eyes, same skin, same hair. Guess maybe it's better in some ways, to be so close in age? Huh?"

What was he seeing in his mind? Pillow fights and makeovers. Me and her doing each other's nails, wearing each other's clothes? Blending into each other the way day moves into night? What Susie imagines about my mother and me is almost true, but the parts he doesn't see are truer.

"She's still my *mom*," I told him.

"Yes she is, Little Miss," he said. "But what does that make *me*?"

It sounds like he's flirting, but I don't think he is. To me it sounds more like stuff he says to make sure I don't feel left out. Maybe he's right, and this is something I need. The way he is when they're in the same room together pushes me to the edges, to a place that isn't really the outside but feels as good as. Like I'm mostly forgotten in this time. Watching him and my mom, it makes my stomach clench.

I don't say much to Susie yet. New friends are harder to read. They might start off nice, easy-going, even fun, but sometimes they have a way of changing. It can start as small as a twitch. A flash. The way they show the thoughts within. A tensing somewhere supposed to be hidden, flickering to the front. Too quick to catch if you're not watching for it.

I've been there before.

Uncle Dan, it was the way he raised his index finger at me one day when he caught me going through his magazines. Babes with bulbous breasts and plastic eyelashes, fingers making Vs between their legs to show the pink inside. Their dumb doll faces oblivious to all the scribbling he'd done on their bodies, eyes scratched out and sternums split with red and black pens. Scissor stitch-marks around their nipples, red ink spirals to show the skin peeling back. He'd pressed down so hard he'd torn the paper in places. He caught me when he wasn't supposed to. His index finger up, stiff and trembling. So desperate to scream at me, he sputtered for a while first. That kind of anger, it has a lot to do with shame.

Uncle Vern, it was in the tilt of his head while he watched me watch TV. Smiling like I was a puppy asleep on the carpet, when really I was just cross-legged on the floor, gaping at the infomercials. When really I was trying to learn about knives, how they cut through leather boots and tin cans like nothing can scratch their metal. When I was thinking how great it would be to have a knife like that of my own. His smile was soft and sappy. The shadows on his face shifting as the light from the TV flickered bright, then dark, and then back again. I saw it all when I turned to look at him, and he stared back at me for the longest time, his hand trembling on his belt buckle, fingers nudging at the tongue. He only looked away in the end because I wouldn't. Staring back at him, thinking about knives while the glare from the TV burned the side of my face.

With Uncle Steve, it was in the first moment when he held his hand out for me to shake. Wrapped his fingers over mine with the smell of bleach and dirty skin. His yellow-toothed grin opening above my head.

I don't like him I don't like him I don't like him.

I don't know why or how I decided so fast. I was too young back then. I didn't know the things I know now.

Susie isn't anything like these other men. I don't know why my mother chose him, but Susie let her choose him, so in some way he must be like the others—or she wouldn't be here. I wouldn't be here. We'd be catching trains inland, we'd be hitchhiking out of the hills. I wouldn't be sleeping on his couch every night with a blanket clenched around my body, which smells like cigarette smoke. I wouldn't be lying awake listening to those staccato slapping sounds, the squeaking bed, those overblown moans coming from the next room. I wouldn't be lying awake all those hours afterward, listening for the sound of bare feet stepping softly down the passage toward me.

4

NO MATTER HOW clearly I see it all in my mind, I'm not always sure how true what my mother tells me really is. How bad it was, I mean. Memories have a way of getting uglier when they're of someone or something we don't like. It's not like my mother starved to death, or lost her teeth from malnutrition when she was carrying me, or died giving birth to me, so she must've had some kind of help. That Man must've been doing something for her. For us. Or, someone had to.

The way she talks, the way she changes . . . I don't always know what to believe.

"Well, there was your Auntie Clem, of course," Momma says. "When I first found out I was pregnant . . . You can't imagine how I felt. I was very young, and very alone. A stupid kid about to have a kid. I understood enough to be scared of you. You were this major thing about to happen to me, and I had no idea what I was supposed to do about you. I wanted to kill myself just to get out of it all. I even mixed up a bottle of bleach and traded a neighbor for a bunch of sleeping pills, but I knew if I went through with it, it would mean killing you, too. Without Auntie Clem . . . " and she smiles the kind of smile that hurts. "Without her, I might've done it anyway."

I do remember this conversation—in fact, this one always

comes back sharp and clear—because it's not often we get to talk about Auntie Clem. We were sitting at a rest stop while the coach we'd been riding ambled off around the corner. We were halfway between one place and another, but I don't recall what we were leaving or where we were headed. Some city, some town. They tend to blur together. We sat at one of the picnic tables—one furthest from the roadside, one with the wider view. Shock-blue sky and crickets buzzing down the banks. We unwrapped our tuna rolls; the cheap kind you buy on-board if you've forgotten to bring something yourself. They come in plastic wrap so thin it's always ripped with holes. Inside, it's stale crust and inside that the bread is soggy. The filling has more mayonnaise than fish.

"You know how big tuna are?" she said through a mouthful, inspecting the bite mark she'd made. Soft center all torn up. "They're really huge, and really shiny. Pretty. It's a shame to turn such a big, beautiful fish into something gross like this."

I stared at mine. A mess of wet whiteness.

"Go on. Eat."

I took a mouthful. Dry bread, fishy-sweet. "But what exactly did Auntie Clem *do*? I mean, how did she—?"

"Don't talk with your mouth full, babe," she said.

I swallowed, and stared past her. A boy sat at the table behind her, reading a book while he ate his roll. Dark eyes, dark hair, olive skin. Solo traveler. Older than me, though not by much. He was listening to an old Walkman, the headphones half-hidden by sharp spikes of gelled hair, the silver band crossing his crown like a metal hinge. Something about this, and the way the light hit his skin in its smooth glow, made him seem unreal. Like he really was made of plastic and metal, the headphones really were a clasp and his head really could open up. And if I opened it I'd see a million tiny cogs and wheels working away in there, forming all his thoughts.

Automaton boy reads book. Automaton boy does not look up at human girl.

He smiled at something on the page.

My mother turned, following my gaze over her shoulder. She looked back at me and raised an eyebrow. I stared down at the roll in my hands, my stomach twisting.

"Auntie Clem got me out of there," she said after a moment. "She got *us* out of there. She didn't have to, but she did. She brought us to her place in Carris, and she gave us a home when we had nowhere left to go." She sighed. "I thought she was an angel for that. For the longest time. I *thought*. A true-blue fucking *angel*."

In my head, I picked at the word *thought*. How vile it sounded in her mouth. I echoed the word *angel*. Said like something she had to spit to get rid of.

"But she *did* still help, didn't she?"

My mother stared. Almost a glare, but not for me. Something inside her, biting, showing its teeth in her eyes. "However it happened, however it turned out, your Auntie Clem put us on the track to finding something far better than the life we would've had otherwise. It didn't happen the way she would've thought, or even wanted, but it still happened. Take the good with the bad, babe."

Automaton Boy looked across at me then, hair throwing a shadow over his eyes. Dark throwing dark over darkness. He stared at me, staring back.

"For all we've done and all we have," my mother said, "this is a pretty good life we've got going here. We're free this way, babe. It's you and me."

Automaton Boy smiled at me then; a slow shifting that stretched the edges of his mouth. A million tiny muscles twitched up and down my back.

***

"We are citizens of this earth," my mother says. "We are Earthlings. That means there's no corner of the planet where we shouldn't be allowed. There isn't a place on the face of it we don't have the right to call *home*."

Momma says when I was younger, in those first months of just her and me, I made her cry sometimes. The way I wouldn't stop talking about Auntie Clem and our home in Carris. Not even trying to fight my dumb little-kid rages, my stubborn child mind. Momma says kids don't realize how much they hurt their parents. She says being a parent is always about being hurt by your kids or hurting for your kids. She says this side of it never stops.

I know I wasn't born in Carris, but I don't remember much of anything about where we lived before Auntie Clem took us in. Mom says before Auntie Clem got us out of there, we stayed in her hometown until I was almost three. She won't give me the exact name. Sometimes she says it's New Richmond, sometimes Gully Ridge, sometimes Harrow. Once she even told me it was 'a town called Despair', but I think she must've been kidding. Her eyes were bright and sharp as she said it, the way they are when she's trying to joke about something that makes her sad. Shards of ice lost in warm water.

When we left Carris, I was still too small to understand. I hadn't learned yet that where you go to sleep isn't always where you wake up, and the people you let yourself love won't always be there again tomorrow. Little kids choose what they want to hear, though they aren't great at listening anyway. I guess I was at that age. Hands over ears, screams. Thrashing at answers like the truth is some kind of attack. Some sort of outrage.

Can we go back? When are we going back?

Wanting Auntie Clem to do my hair for me. Make French toast for me. Wanting her to choose my clothes or tie a shoe or take me to the bathroom.

I don't wanna go with you.

I said that. On a day I don't remember, when momma tells me I kicked and screamed and tried to punch her, my face bunched tight and darkened red like 'a dried-up tomato'.

A dried-up tomato.

What a hideous face. My face? I don't want to picture it. Little girls should never be terrors, no matter how afraid they are, or how angry they feel. Tantrums, rages, screams. It doesn't fit right—so much ugliness blasting out from a blonde-haired thing in pretty clothes. If this is what being spoiled can turn a child into, then I'm glad we've never stayed anywhere too long since. I'm glad Auntie Clem's house was the last place I thought we'd be forever.

There isn't anywhere on the face of the Earth that we don't have the right to call home.

Each new landscape and all its characters temporary to us. Like touring a souvenir shop, like flicking through a set of Polaroids. Fascinating things, beautiful things, and all shuffled in with the things you can't wait to forget. Because not all the places we pass through are fascinating, beautiful. Sometimes we leave with the metal-panic taste of blood and adrenalin thick in our saliva, lights in our eyes that set to spinning in flares of crazy, urgent red. Everything screaming so loud it feels like violence, those pulses, those bursts.

This isn't real, I know, but it's how it feels.

My momma has a way of knowing when it's time for us to go. The older I get, the more I feel it too. A sense of tension tightens in, starts to swell in the air. It's like slow suffocation. For days something unnamable skims all the surfaces, sets fire to our nerves.

That man has been following us.
That woman keeps looking at us.
Who is he calling?

What is she writing down?

Everything, the smallest thing, feels like a warning, some kind of sign. A sudden cloudburst. A late train. A broken zipper. Malicious. Vicious. Cruel. Our guts churn while we sleep so we wake in sick panic every morning.

Get up. Get up!

All the times this has happened before. My mother's hurried whisper close to my ear, raking me out of sleep. Her cool hands trembling as she brushes the hair out of my face, opens her palms and pats my cheeks.

Wake up honey. Please. Let's go.

And it's the paranoia that makes us rush, move. Grab what we can and be gone before the sun splits the dark lines of the horizon and the sky.

We are citizens of this earth.

Which is another way to say, there's no one place where my momma and me really belong.

5

WHEN WE GET back 'home'—Susie's home, more a collection of random furniture and broken knick-knacks crammed within solid walls than it is a 'home'—my mother shrugs off her jacket and throws it on the kitchen table. I set down the milk, the eggs and lube I carried under my own jacket. I keep the two packs of gum in my back pocket. Those are for me.

"We didn't think to take any bread," my mother says. She rolls her eyes at me, smiling.

Aren't we silly? that smile says.

I sit down at the table and watch her as she moves through the unfamiliar kitchen, checking cupboards and drawers and back shelves. She finds a frying pan, a bottle of sunflower oil. A brick of cheese at the back of the fridge wrapped in grease-paper and mummified to something hard that crumbles to shards when she breaks off a corner.

"Parmesan," she smiles at me. Maybe it is and maybe it isn't.

She makes us scrambled eggs. Soft yellow lumps spiced with finely grated cheese. We eat in silence. Each mouthful is smooth and warm and familiar. The way my mother makes eggs: she gets them perfect every time. Never too

25

raw and never too rubbery. Somehow they always taste the same, no matter how dirty the kitchen or how bare the supplies.

My mother, sometimes she can make anything beautiful.

***

We're asleep watching TV when Susie gets back. My head in my mother's lap, lost in something dreamless. When I slide awake it's because the door opened at the wrong time in the sitcom jingle, and then slammed, and the sound was coming from behind us, not the TV. I keep my eyes closed, feel the rush of air and catch the shush of movement as he steps around the couch, then crouches down in front of us. I don't know where he's looking. If it's at me, or at my mother. Or if his eyes are moving between the two of us, comparing and contrasting. What's the same and what's different. What's better, what's not.

After a moment, he sighs. There's a hard tap and light clatter as he swipes the remote off the coffee table, a pop into sudden silence when he switches the TV off. My mother shifts and sighs, ready to wake up—or feign waking up, because I'm sure she was listening just as hard as me.

"Hey sleeping beauties," Susie says. His voice is soft as sandpaper dusting raw wood—smooth, careful. Not rough or sharp or fast. "Come on," he says. "Let's get you in bed."

***

When I wake up, I'm not always sure where I am. The places we sleep aren't permanent the way it is for people in movies and, I guess, real life. Their beds, their covers, their cushions. The feel of the mattress, the angle of the light. They can wake up and stand up and still know where they are, even in pitch darkness. In the movies, the guys grope for baseball bats stashed under their beds. Women fumble for a light switch, a phone, whatever they need that's on the nightstand. Like they know it will be there, because they put it there.

When I was little, I peed in closets and corners, too desperate and confused by the strange layout of rooms to know where the bathroom was. Too lost in strange dark. Now I know to hold it. In desperation, I once peed in a coffee mug. A dog food bowl. A kitchen sink.

Susie's place is small, easy to navigate. There aren't as many rooms to zigzag your sense of where things should be. If I peed in his coffee mug, it would be on purpose. If I peed in the corner, it would be out of spite.

I've mostly seen this town at dawn, at night. Susie's house is a few blocks from the train station. It's an easy morning walk down the deserted streets. Calm and quiet through the still darkness, a time when people speak in whispers even if there's nobody else around. I like this town. I like the morning walk. My trappers boots—my new favorite shoes, bought for me at a city store six months ago—are smooth and quiet. Thick rubber, soft steps. My mother walks in ballet slippers, flat-footed so she can stretch her calves, her heels stuffed in her bag for later. We walk in the middle of the road, following the smooth black tar, the barrier line shining white between us. It's too early for cars. Still, it always feels so daring—walking where people are not supposed to walk. The zippers and straps on our bags jingle. A few birds sing, their calls louder than they are when the sun is up and the traffic is thick and the world is all the way awake. I like the town like this; I wouldn't want to see so much of it during the day, away from this easy calm, this cool air. The sun brings chaos; it changes everything. I sometimes don't know myself: the ways I am, day from night.

Momma and me don't talk a lot so early in the day. We're still half-dreaming, the world *other* enough at that hour for us to half-believe the inner landscapes we've just left are sort of real—hill giants and secret histories and all. Sleep-sight tainting reality. A surreal mist, sliding over.

The walk from Susie's house to the train station is twelve minutes, the way we go. A suburban backroad, a stretch of open path, then out onto the street that bends past the entrance in a staggered U. By the time we reach it, the day noises are catching up and the sky is brightening. We grab some coffee from the kiosk, we get our tickets. We board the first train, always almost empty, and I stretch out on the three-seater with my head in my mother's lap. I drift inside the smells of coffee, perfume, cigarette smoke. Disinfectant. Scents caught in the fabric of her clothes, trapped in her hair, caught in the seats. I'll be dozing when the train moves off—that gentle lurch before it starts rolling sets me straight to sleep again, or holds me down in the place in-between.

Sometimes falling asleep and waking up feel a lot the same.

The way a train moves, it's like being rocked very gently. There's a faint whirring sound, it speeds up into a rhythm, a steady staccato that moves up from underneath and paves the way for dreams.

I don't dream so much, or so easily, in a stranger's bed or on a stranger's couch. Sleep in those places is greyed out, solid, featureless. Like running into a wall and knocking yourself out. So different to when I'm curled up on a coach liner or dozing with my head pressed to a rubber-sealed window, the buzz of turning wheels vibrating through my skull in a constant, swift tremor. Real sleep—and dreams—are easier for me when we're in motion. My mother jokes if I ever napped on a surfboard out at sea, I'd dream in technicolor.

The people in my dreams come in fragments. Like portraits cut into puzzle pieces and then scattered, only the pictures sometimes move. A shoulder sticking out from behind a tree, elbow at an arc. Eyes watching me from secret places, sometimes wide and blinking, sometimes glassy and staring-white like smoky marbles. Or I only find signs of people—people who've just been here, people I've missed by bare moments. A loud conversation, echoing incoherent from across an unknown space. Excited or angry, I can't tell. Footsteps in black mud, bare or booted, pressed deep and cut clear by the weight that made them. In my dreams, there are no buildings. I see open parking lots scattered with abandoned cars. I see sidewalk spaces, gutters, cutting through forests and fields of flowers. If I see a door, it opens to a hole in the ground. In the real world there are stories about these doors. Usually they're stories about fairies. I know from those stories if you go through that kind of door you don't always get to come out. I never open them, and those are the only doors I find in my dreams. I don't dream about apartment blocks or backyards. I don't see entrance halls or cottage steps. It's like in my dreams, nothing that might have walls exists.

My mother's right. *Home* for us doesn't have to be a fixed place. I find it in slots of time, in slants of light. I feel it closest at dawn, when night and day meld and mingle a while before they drift apart. Home for me is my head in my mother's lap, and those dreamscapes I see before I'm all the way awake. My jacket wrapped tight around me and my boots up on the seats. The tastes of toothpaste and coffee cloudy on the back of my tongue, the soft sweep of my mother's fingers sliding through my hair. It's me knowing, *I can sleep a while longer.* Thinking, *I don't have to open my eyes just yet.*

There's a safe space there, in the pauses between words. Comfortable and familiar as the shape of my mother's thighs, tensed beneath my head.

6

SUSIE HAS A laptop, like the one I want one day. Silver and flat with keys that light up. I want to learn how to type, when I'm older. I want to teach my fingers to move that fast. My eyes fixed on the words in front of me. Those messages I see.

Susie doesn't have a dog, but I think he's the type who'd suit one. Something big and burly up on the couch with him, his arm slung around snug shoulders. His fingers rubbing a soft ear in slow circles. I know how it might feel.

I can't find Susie's porn collection. I guess it's on the laptop, but I don't know the password. I've searched everywhere for magazines—I want to know what type he'd buy. Ball gags and whips, wide eyes streaming tears, bulging at the choke. There's a kind of man who likes this look—tears black with mascara, streaking down soft cheeks. That kind of man: you can't always tell. Maybe he goes for the blonde types, pink types, the types who giggle a lot and pretend they don't understand. I guess so, looking at my mother, and the way he looks at her, especially when she's playing stupid. My mother's breasts aren't fake and she says I ruined them, but I've never seen a man who wasn't working hard to get a better view. Even when her hair is platinum. Even when she's dyed it black.

Susie has a small silver circle at the top of his left ear.

Punched right through the cartilage, so you know it had to hurt. My momma hasn't let me get my ears pierced yet. She says earrings look trashy on little girls.

Even though I'm not little anymore.

Susie doesn't have a dog, but he says he'll get one.

I can't ask him about his porn collection, and I won't ask him about the laptop. I don't know what would happen if he offered to buy me one. What he might ask me for in return, I mean.

7

THE LONGEST WE ever stayed put in one place was from when I was a toddler to around age five, six at most. Old enough to remember, but not in any solid kind of way. That place in small-town Carris. Our smallholding on the edge of a rural, mountain-locked valley. If I hear or say the word *home*, this is what I remember. The house, the driveway, the trees. Like a house in a forest, except for the road. The summer thunderstorms, and the way the roof creaked. The warmth inside, burning out.

"Each memory you hold is just a moment that's already passed," my mom says. "The only way to be happy in life is to live in the *now*."

She would look wise saying this if it wasn't for her smile. Goofy, with squinted eyes and tongue caught between her teeth. It means she's planning something, about to say something completely different, because really she's desperate to change the subject.

" . . . and *now*, I say we go get doughnuts."

" . . . and *now*, I say we find out how many channels our Man of the Moment's TV here has."

" . . . and *now*, I say we raid the liquor cabinet and go check out the pool."

So we live in the now. Like one of those guru dudes on

late-night TV once said. *Live in the Now.* Making the words echo, backlighting them in spirals of blue and a million tiny flashes.

While I don't know much about before, I do remember Carris. Or, the sense of it. In a way, I remember our time there like it somehow got burned into me, scars beneath my skin I have to touch and manipulate to find the breadth of them.

You can take a thick, black marker and swipe a big, bold line straight through my life at exactly this split: the time when we were at Carris, and the time after we left. Draw the line like a cliff-edge, straight down ragged and steep and without place for pause. Because it really was like that. Looking at the Before and then at the After, there is no in-between.

***

In those early years, I thought my momma and Auntie Clem and me were the only real people on earth. I thought it was only the three of us who had ideas and feelings. Lives. A crazy kid-belief that all the other folks around were more like automatons than real people. They appeared as we drove into town and then took their positions, played their roles, followed their cues. Everyone we ever saw, whether we knew their names or not. The shop people in town who rang up and bagged our groceries, the guy at the filling station who checked our tires and cleaned our windscreen, the people strolling around with bags in their hands. Standing in clusters, making small-town chitchat. Their actions and movements and words scripted by something Other, recited entirely just for us. When we drove back home after a trip into town, the backseat crammed with shopping bags, me riding shotgun on Momma's lap, I imagined a dusty darkness enveloping the space behind us the moment it was out of view. A cloud storm of nothingness overwhelming everything, stripping it back to blankness. A void that would stay empty until the next time we approached it, when the smoke would swirl into something solid and again form the rest of the world.

What I mean is, there's a part of me even now that isn't sure anyone I meet is actually real. I am, I know. I've felt my heart choke its way up my throat, and I've seen myself bleed. I know what it is to be alone with my thoughts. They're real, even if no-one else can look into my mind and read the things I see in here. And I know Momma's real, because if she's not real then nothing is. Not even me.

I have something else, too. A third eye set into my forehead, secret and unseen. It sits a half inch above the bridge of my nose. It's big and it's round, and it's the deepest, glossiest black. It shines like it's wet, even though I've never cried out of it. It's not an eye I use like a normal eye. Most of the time it keeps itself closed, and when it's closed my flesh-and-blood eyes are open. When it's open, my normal eyes are shut. What my real eyes show me and what this other eye says is real don't always match. The way a black and white photograph and its color version can't be considered identical, even though they're both of the same thing and were taken at the same time. Sometimes that eye stays open too long, and when it finally closes my normal eyes have trouble recognizing where I am, or who's around me. The room I'm in might be different. The way I'm lying might have changed. I suddenly have something over me—a blanket, a coat—or something taken away. Sometimes I have marks on my body—around my wrists, on the insides of my thighs. My neck will hurt like I've been sleeping wrong for hours without shifting once, the way it is when you fall asleep on a coach in a seat without a proper headrest. I guess when you sleep, your body is not your own.

It's not so important, what's real and what's not, what's true and what isn't. It all changes from moment to moment. The road you were just on will vanish behind, and what follows is a dust storm that takes everything over. There's no point looking back. It's not there anymore, anyway.

Still. Even when my two normal eyes are open and I'm all the way here and all the way aware, I sense my black eye pulsing. It's like an itch in the bone, this feeling. Rolling over, buzzing in slow circles. Like a wasp's nest boiling in honey. Angry. It shows me blood. It sprays a stench of scarlet across people's faces as they're talking to me. It drags claws through their eyes. It hurts them, shreds them. I have to watch it like a psychic death-wish. Sick and surreal as a 70s horror film, like the ones that dude by the coast made us watch. I had to pretend I didn't like them, but I did. What my eye shows me makes me feel the same.

Sometimes I think I keep my head down so much out of a kind of instinct—a fear that someone will look at my forehead, and see the sleeping eye I'm hiding there. I keep my head down so my hair falls in my face. I keep my shoulders up so nobody can glance around my edges. Maybe it's good I do this, maybe it's even important. Because when I catch strangers staring at me a certain way—motherly and soft, full of concern and questions—that eye seethes like a thing catching fire. Like it wants to do all my seeing for me. And I don't know what would happen if I allowed this to happen, but I do know the idea scares me. Worried my usual eyes will die if I allow it, roll right out of my skull and melt down my cheeks, and I won't be able to see anything solid or colorful ever again. Every stranger a monster. Every smile grotesque.

8

THE CITY WE'RE visiting today, it's one we've been to before. At least, that's what my mother tells me. We must've last been here when I was still really young. It has a few streams and canals zigzagging through it. It has unusually narrow roads. There aren't as many tall buildings, not over six stories anyway, and a lot of people ride around on bicycles. It's pretty, but kind of worn down, run down, trash in the gutters and faded posters on the lampposts and outer shop walls, half-torn and weathered.

"Let's see if we can find it," my mother says.

We've been walking this street a long time now, following the fence with its line of trees, looking for the entrance to the park. The fencing that surrounds it has been erected flush against the original low stone walls; a high crisscross brace of metal with barbed wire nesting along the top. Maybe there are problems with crime in the area at night. Probably the park has only two workable entrances now, one on either end. And it's a big park. We could be walking for ages, following the fence along this road.

"I'm pretty sure it was this one," she says. "There's a lake thing in there somewhere. Really more of a big pond pretending to be a lake. I took you one morning to go feed the ducks."

"Ducks?" I say. It feels like a word I don't know.

Mom takes my arm and laughs. "*Ducks*. Why do you say it like *that*?"

"I don't remember any ducks."

"But you *loved* the ducks." Her grip on my arm tightens. "I had to keep you from running out into the water to play with them. I think that's why we had to leave, actually. Stubborn, crazy little girl. You wouldn't listen to your momma."

She laughs, her hand slips down to mine and she raises my palm to her mouth for a quick kiss. Then she lets me go.

It's a chilly morning out here and my jacket is too thin. I wrap my arms around my ribs.

"Come on, girl." My mother's elbow nudges me. "Try to look more open. You're slouching."

This slouching thing, it's not the same as when my head drops down and my hair falls in my face. About a year ago, my height finally crept up to meet my mother's, and then began to take over. I'm a full inch taller than her now, which is bad, and I know it's bad from the way my mother keeps promising me—herself?—that I must be done growing now, that this is the tallest I will ever be, because my body has to stop sometime and now is definitely the time.

When I step too close beside my mother, it's like my shoulders fold in. Away from her.

'Pretty girls should never walk like they're ashamed of what they've got.'

It's one thing to hide my forehead, it's another thing to hide my height. Even if I'm taller than I should be, hunching over never looks nice. When I remember, I drop my arms again. I keep my shoulders back.

My mother walks and stands and laughs and talks like she's nothing but busting with pride over every little thing she's ever been and ever done, like everything beautiful we see around us is all her own doing. People feel this energy. Even surly-looking strangers catch themselves easing up to her. She's like a swirl of warm water rolling through the cold. There's a casual brightness to her that puts people at ease when they're edgy, lifts them out of themselves when they're guarded. Like she challenges them to be free.

It's something I feel too sometimes, watching her.

The road curves left up ahead, and by the way the traffic has been thickening up to it I guess we're heading toward an intersection or something. Fewer pedestrians, more bikes and scooters. Mini-sized cars, buses, lumbering in-between.

"I think I remember this," my mother says. Her steps slow, she looks around. The wind whips her hair and sends a strand into her open mouth. She tears it away, red fingernails raking her cheek. Her smile widens. "There was a concession stand or something just up around this corner. A man selling pastries and coffee. I got you a hot chocolate and a cinnamon twist. Do you remember?"

I don't remember the ducks. I don't remember wanting to chase them into the lake. Or play with them, whatever. I don't remember anything about a man with hot chocolate and pastries. I'm not like my mother. I don't remember everything.

She puts her arm through mine again. As we follow the bend, the view opens up to a three-way intersection with zebra-stripe crossings and bus lanes and bike lanes. The metal fencing links up to a gated entrance, now wide open. There's a kiosk—not a concession stand exactly but a brick and paint hut thing—exhaling the scents of coffee and chocolate and warm sugar from its open-shuttered window.

"I knew it," Mom squeals, jumping up and down on the balls of her feet. "I knew it!"

I smile because suddenly it does look familiar, and warm,

and sort of cheerful. I smile because younger-me was here once, short stubby legs clunking around in gumboots, tiny hand held tight in younger-hers as we stood at this kiosk and she ordered a coffee for her and a hot chocolate for me, and a cinnamon twist for the both of us. For some reason, I'm pretty sure about the gumboots, even if I'm not totally sold on the hot chocolate. Would I remember that? I think they were pink, with white daisies and *Hello Kitty* all over them. Or they were the usual dark green, or black.

Actually, I have no idea.

"You wanna feed the ducks?" she turns to me, smiling with her tongue caught between her teeth. "No swimming this time, though, okay?"

The way she nudges me as she says this, it makes me laugh.

"Come on, little duck-lover."

We walk past the kiosk, and the guy is doing something with steam and taps. The thing he's turning screech-hisses in his hands, hot like it hurts. The steam hits his face and the skin slides away in thinning layers. I don't know if he smiles at me, but he's grinning.

***

Parks with lakes in them always feel sort of stiff, because they're the kind adults like just as much as kids. There are couples walking around holding hands. Some are teenagers, palms locked with bent wrists like they don't know if it's okay to touch each other yet. Some are really old—slow steps, tight-clasped arms. There are lone people, too. Men in suits sit on benches overlooking the water. They have backpacks or laptop cases resting beside them. Many sit with an arm through the strap, I guess to make sure nothing valuable will get snatched away from them in some random, terrible moment. They sit and stare across the lake while they talk on their phones, sip coffee out of branded cups. And some of them sit staring at their hands, at their feet, at something lost somewhere in front of them. There are lone women, too, though not so many. I take a moment to notice one woman, early thirties with neat hair and wearing one of those tight-cut suit jacket things. She stands close to the water, elbows resting on the iron railing. I can tell by the way she stands that she's nervous, unsure. Her back is too straight, her legs are too stiff. Her lips keep twitching like she's having a conversation with herself in her head, and some of it is leaking through.

God knows what it is she's thinking. God knows the things people say to themselves.

"It's busy here," I say to mom. "Not too many kids, either."

I'm wearing makeup today. There are times and places where my mom wants me to, and times and places where she definitely doesn't. The beauty of my baby-face and my fast-developed body, you see, is my flexible age. Choose between a ponytail or a blow wave. A pink tracksuit top or a short denim skirt. Add or remove makeup and I can go between a tall twelve to a cool seventeen and back again in just one wardrobe change.

Of course, I learned this watching her. Of course, we learned how to do this together.

"Maybe they got rid of the ducks," my mother says.

But who cares about the *ducks*?

The lake is flat and green. It smells foul, secret. Like something hidden is rotting somewhere. A low, dank stench trails off the water. It makes me think of fish paste and pickled beetroot. I'm shivering because the water chills the air and my jacket is too thin.

We take a long, slow walk across the park, following the water from one end to the other. There are a few security guys, but they seem to stick closer to the entrances. The public toilets dotted throughout are each set further back, behind the trees, almost out of sight from the water but not so hidden that they're difficult to find. We find the place where the ducks hang out—by a curved wooden jetty type thing leading out over the water. They're cute, I guess—the ducks—but I don't remember them. We pass more people as we explore. They give us brief glances as they stroll by. Nobody here seems big on eye contact with strangers.

No one really *looks* at us, I mean.

"It's not the same as it was," my mother says. "Not even close." A little worried. "Maybe some kids drowned here or something. For starters there was no railing around the water last time. And the place feels less . . . less . . . "

"Kid friendly?"

"Exactly." She turns for a moment to study my face. "Something feels wrong," she says.

I've got two stiff, square envelopes jammed down the backs of my jeans pockets. There's nowhere else to put them because my jacket is too thin and it's one of those fashion-focused things with mock-pockets—zips that open and close but lead to nowhere, contain nothing. Right about now, I'm starting to feel just as useless.

"Are we poor again, Momma?" I say to her. Something is gripping my stomach. Panic stings my nerves, flaring in my fingertips like I've touched a flame.

"Hey, kid, we always make a plan," she says. She's using her low voice, the soothing one I don't hear very often. It's one she uses to reassure me. But I know her—I know she wouldn't talk like this if she wasn't worried herself. "We're just getting a handle on things here. There's always Susie for now."

Susie. He seems to like her enough and accept me okay enough, but is it really *enough*? And even if it is, how long can we trust it to last?

She stops us walking, turns and cups my hands together in hers. "Can I leave you alone for a while?"

Something hideous prickles across my scalp and all at once my jacket isn't too thin anymore—all at once I'm boiling and I want to rip the thing off my shoulders so I can breathe.

"Not now, please, Momma. It doesn't feel . . . I can't . . . "

She looks at me for a moment, her beautiful, arched eyes deep with worry. "It's up to you, doll," she says. "You know I'll always leave it up to you."

Sometimes when I look at my face in the mirror, that look she has in her eyes right now is exactly the same as I see in my own. The desire for home, the hunger for safety. The exhaustion we feel, living in chaos.

See the good with the bad.

You know I'll always leave it up to you.

And knowing every time I say *No* is one day more, before we'll finally have a place of our own.

9

I DON'T KNOW anything about my real dad, but if you can make a woman a father I think maybe Auntie Clem was this for me. She was my mother-father, which still makes me lucky, because not all kids get to have a father, male or female. Not even for a while. Sometimes having one wouldn't be so good for them anyway. I can say this from being in other kid's houses. Going through their drawers and cupboards. Sleeping in their beds.

A unicorn diary with a lock that popped right open. I didn't even have to search for the key. Those pages full of looping, curling handwriting, hearts hovering above all the 'i's', spelling out sad words.

A plastic Tupperware stashed under a bed, filled with moldy cupcakes and half-opened chocolate slabs, all the edges nibbled at like a night squirrel with clever hands. The word PIGLET taped to the lid, scrawled out in big block letters. Not my box and not my name, but even I felt a little insulted.

Once, when staying the night in a boy's room, I peeled back a Carmen Electra poster and the words SHIT and FUCK screamed out at me from that hidden square of wall. Written over and over with different types of pens, the lettering both small and big, scratched and scrawled with such heat I was scared to touch anything, to feel how deep the words had been scored. Scared I might catch whatever was burning there.

Maybe I was lucky, having Auntie Clem instead of a dad.

"Little girl," she called me, roughing a heavy hand through my hair. "Angel kid."

Auntie Clem was a big woman with powerful shoulders and a wide chest shaped like an oak barrel—the way the bones curved out under layers of tough muscle, her breasts sliding around on the surface in two flat pouches of unanchored flesh. Her small, puffy hands were always dry and cracked. She bit her nails and the skin around them, turning her fingertips into rough, ragged things that scratched when she tickled me. Auntie Clem laughed like a man and talked like a man. She hugged me hard and kissed me harder, picking me up and throwing me over her shoulder so I squealed laughter, the blood thickening in my face like strawberry syrup. I was always kind of scared of her, as much as I loved being around her. Her big, fish-lipped smile. Her laugh like exploding granite. Those hands that held too hard and left bruises, even though they only touched me in love.

Is this what having a father is like? A good one, I mean?

The house the three of us lived in belonged to her—much of the surrounding property, too. It had been left to her by a brother or a dead husband, I don't know for sure, I never got this straight and I can't ask about it now. Auntie Clem might have been my mother's cousin, or maybe she was just an old friend, though sometimes when they were drinking wine and holding hands across the kitchen table, crying, they said they were sisters.

I can't ask about this now, either.

While I don't remember the time before Carris myself, I picked up a few clues along the way. Things my mom and Auntie Clem said to each other in low voices, guarding how sad and secret the facts were. Like saying it louder would give it teeth and claws and let it loose to hurt us. I heard the things they said when they thought I wasn't listening, and the things they said when they knew I was.

Sitting at the scarred kitchen table in low light, late at night, Momma and Auntie Clem talked a lot about 'growing up too fast' and 'staying sane'. They talked about the past tearing up the backs of their legs like rabid poodles—scary, noisy little things that can only do you damage if you turn to face their fangs. But when they said these things they were talking about themselves, each other, and not about me.

"Children deserve a shot at staying innocent," I remember Auntie Clem saying to my momma.

"It doesn't last so long, anyway," my momma said.

"Don't we know it."

And when they said these things, sometimes it was me they were talking about, but really they were still talking about themselves.

Auntie Clem worked for a trucking company. Not driving the trucks but doing something else with them that called her away for weeks at a time. Momma and me kept the house going while she was gone. We kept it clean and we fixed what got broken and we spent hours at the kitchen table with paper and colored pencils and alphabet books and picture books and puzzles and wooden blocks and tiny plastic farm animals I got to move around. The way I learned to count and multiply, the way I learned to read and write, I never understood it was anything else than just a game we were playing. A game my momma had invented, for her and me alone.

I'm told I'm lucky because I got to learn without knowing I was learning. No noisy classrooms, no boys pulling my hair, no screaming teachers or playground traumas. No friends, no class parties, no paper airplanes or passed notes or sleepover invites, either. I don't know if school really is like any of this. I only know about these things the way movies and TV shows tell them.

The house on the property was old and big and a little too close to rundown. I see that now, looking back, remembering the damp stains spreading down the faded wallpapered walls, the way the kitchen taps shook and sometimes spat rust when we opened them. The weak spots on the hardwood floors we knew not to step on. I slept in what Auntie Clem called 'the back bedroom', the one furthest from hers and my mother's. It had a small desk, a bookshelf, a prince bed pushed up against the single large sash window. No curtains. At night I'd lie and stare up at the sky through the glass; the thick, black web of tree branches veined over the stars. That natural kind of darkness. The sun would wake me up in the early hours, white-bright the way it is when it's still flush against the horizon, warming my sheets until I started to sweat under there. And so when I got up, I slid out from under damp, stuffy covers and stepped into cool, night-touched air.

Even now, if I have a choice, I prefer to sleep without covering the windows.

The property was one of a widely-spaced handful, all joined by a single dirt road. A school bus went by that way, and sometimes it passed me as I was standing near the gate, kicking stones over or looking for frogs or whatever. The bus wasn't a bus like you see in movies. It was more of a van, a twelve-seater or something. And it was white, with CARRIS PUBLIC SERVICES stenciled on the side in black. Carris was so small it didn't need its own dedicated school bus. The van had a lot of different jobs. It shuttled the folks at the old age home in and out of town to do their weekly shopping; transported new convicts to the nearest max-security prison a few hours away; it was a makeshift ambulance for the local doctor's rooms, and there must've been a dozen more uses for it. It went to a lot of different places. It carried a lot of different types of people. But when it was a school bus, there were children inside of it. Neon pink and bright yellow backpacks. Rows of small, pony-tailed heads. Braces and buzz-cuts and too-loud voices whipping through the open windows as the van bumped by, its wheels churning up dense billows of fine red dust.

Once or twice a kid would see me, and wave as they passed. A small hand pressed to a grease-smeared pane, a salute across the wind, there and gone. I remember jumping up and down once, grinning, waving back. But the van went by and the brake lights didn't flare red and a few moments later it had vanished over the hill, ready to turn onto the tar road that wove toward the high street and behind, to the school.

School.

"I'm home-schooling you," Mom told me. "You don't need to go to a school with other kids, with strangers all around you."

Children deserve a shot at staying innocent.

I wanted a bright pink backpack. I wanted to tie my hair up in a ponytail with a puffy, polka-dot hairband like one I'd once seen. I wanted to sit in the van and press my hand to the window, waving at any other little kids we passed. Little kids who stood staring, envious of kids like me who got to stay home instead.

It doesn't last so long, anyway.

"I want you to stay away from the road," my mother said. "It's not safe for you."

Don't we know it.

You might think she meant it wasn't safe for me to be in the road, even though it was a quiet one and not many vehicles went by. All the same. The way she said the words 'not safe' gave me visions of a roaring monster with flashing eyes and silver-grill teeth that would catch me up and throw me into the gravel by the roadside. Crack my skull, smash my legs, shatter my ribs. Kill me. I thought that was what she meant by 'not safe'. I thought that for the longest time. But that wasn't what she was worried about. Why would it be, when there was so much more to lose?

10

THE WAY MOMMA and me walk back from the park, it's the way we've walked unfamiliar high streets in the middle of the night. Dusty backroads with no streetlights. Highways that snake ahead to secret places we can't reach. We walk with our arms looped together, our steps skittering in and out of time. She'll squeeze me where she holds me and I'll squeeze her back. She'll nudge me with her elbow and I'll smile. My mom and me, this growing up thing is something we've had to do together. Sometimes we'll walk a long way before we talk.

"Crystal ball, crystal ball . . . " she whispers to me, just loud enough to hear over the background rush of cars and bikes and strangers' footsteps passing back and forth.

"Round and small . . . " I say back.

"What will we have when we have it all?"

I haven't thought about this in a while now. It's been so long since we played this game.

"A house in the woods with a moat all around it," I say. Then think. "No, a house on an island in the middle of a really big lake."

"Why not a mansion?"

"I want something small and cozy," I say. "Something pretty I won't have to work hard to keep clean."

"But won't you have servants to keep it clean?"

"I don't want servants. I want to be all alone. My place, all mine. No-one comes over without my say-so. And I want a big oak tree growing in the garden. With a swing hanging from one of the branches. I'll sit outside and drink champagne under the stars, and then I'll swing until dawn."

"You? All alone? But then where will I stay?"

I have to think about this. "You'll have your own house on the mainland, close to the city, because that's where you want to be. But . . . you'll have a secret rowboat so you can come out and see me anytime you want. You'll be the only one who knows the way to the island. And for you, it'll take no time at all. For anyone else, it'll take forever."

She laughs, half through her nose. "That's cute, kid. Kinda sad, but cute."

"Crystal ball . . . crystal ball . . . " I start.

"Round and small . . . "

"What will we have when we have it all?"

The crystal ball of mine she doesn't know about, it throbs above my eyes as I wait for her to answer.

"A secret rowboat," she says, squeezing my arm and huddling closer to me as we walk. "So I can visit my beautiful, amazing daughter and help her stop feeling so alone."

"No *yacht*?" I say. "No private *helicopter*? No *caviar* pantry and closet full of suede jackets?"

I don't know why I'm angry, but I am.

"Hey now," she says. "Hey . . . "

Usually my momma and me are closest to each other when things go wrong, when we have the world against us and cheering each other up is a game we play. That's not how I feel right now. How I feel now, it's how I felt watching her and Susie dance in his tiny square kitchen a few nights back, his stereo pumping sound from the other room. Old-school rock n' roll, the kinds of songs they play at pool bars when things start to get rowdy. I sat at the table where my momma and me eat scrambled eggs. I watched the two of them as they pushed and pulled and stepped close, and then back, my mother's hair flying across her face when he spun her round. Something in my heart expanding so it pushed against my ribs and my throat. Something that is hard on the outside and hollow on the inside. The bigger it got the more it hurt, echoing and ricocheting inside me. Shoving my heart out the way, trapping the air in my throat.

When can I be like her?

Why can't I be like her?

Dancing happy and free, loose and smooth and lively as a swath of silk floating in a dark tide. Sometimes just watching her makes me feel like a torn-up piece of cardboard, stiff and stinking with forgotten stains. Awkward, heavy, soiled.

"Sorry, Momma," I say now. I try to smile. "PMS or something, I think."

"Oh," she says. "Oh."

She knows it's a lie, has to be.

"I don't need caviar or suede jackets," she says. She's taken the laughter out of her voice. She's talking soft and serious. "I need to know that you're close, safe. You could give me a million crystal balls and a billion wishes. That's all I'd ask for, every time."

She stops walking when she stops talking. She makes me turn to face her. I duck my head, conscious again of my extra inch. My hair falls into my eyes.

"You're my beautiful girl," she says. She closes her arms around me, and leans to kiss me softly on my forehead. My secret eye flickers the instant her lips touch it. I fight the moment. Keeping it closed.

We're blocking the walkway. The strangers passing clip us

at the shoulders. Their annoyance swarms around them and crashes against us as they step by, sighing through their noses like snorting bulls.

It's funny how predictable people are. How easy they are to poke.

"Don't mind them," Momma says, and hugs me tighter.

I don't.

11

You know how *many kids would kill to go on road trips all the time?*

It's not only my mother who's said that. A lot of friends and uncles have, too. I don't know what other kids would feel about it, but I know about me.

Forget *Carris*. Forget *home*. When we're settled in a town or city for too long, I miss the freedom and chaos we find in the wider world. Following the roads, just my momma and me. Deciding a direction by flipping a coin, by dodging the sun, by watching the moon. By spinning around three times with our hands held out in front of us. Stop, stumble, stand. And whichever stretch of horizon we both see, that's the way we go.

I know we're making our plans, I know we're doing what we need to do so we can buy a house one day and never have to ask anyone for money ever again. I know when we reach this place it will be our new forever. But for now, the best part is still how we get there.

Dumping our bags out at bus depots to scratch together loose change. Making up sob-stories to tell sympathetic ticket-sellers. The matronly, lost-cause mother-types usually, in their stretched-out uniforms, with their badly-permed hair.

Or.

Standing at the crossroads with our thumbs out, the wind whipping at my momma's skirt so the guys who don't stop whistle as they roar past, and the guys who do stop open their doors with wide smiles. Shaking their heads at her, at me, like they don't really disapprove at all.

I grew up on strong legs and sore feet from those hours walking strange streets. My arms and face tanned from waiting at the roadside while my momma held out her thumb, her hand trembling against clouds of dust. People who choose not to see us, they have a way of vanishing in blood bursts that dissolve into the air like they never were. Or maybe it's my third eye doing this. It's only the ones who stopped for us, and were nice to us, that I've ever allowed to live. I slept curled up on cigarette-scarred seats with my head in my mother's lap, listening to the wheels roll beneath us as whatever coach we were riding pushed on through the night, the deep choke and change of its engine growling in its mouth. I knew how to read time tables, I got good at counting platform numbers. I got even better at following signs—both the ones on walls and the ones on faces. I figured out from the way people smiled at me which strangers might give me something, and which ones might give my mom money, and which ones had something blank in their faces or dark in their eyes. The ones my mother might want to talk to and those she wouldn't. I learned how to wash my hair in restroom sinks, how to help my momma wash hers so there was no soap left in to make it dry in sticky clumps. How to change my clothes in the backseat of a car or the back row of a bus without anyone noticing. How to fix my mother's eyeliner when there weren't any decent mirrors around.

This is only weird to you if you've grown up some other way.

"I did my best, babe," she's said. "If we were stuck

someplace for a while, like at night, I'd cover you with my coat and put my arm over you, so at a glance people would think you were just luggage. You were so small back then I still could. And I was fine if folks were bothering me. You have to understand, babe. I did my best."

I tell them that.

She did her best.

"People who've never done this think truckers and lone travelers who pick up hitchhikers are all bad, scary monsters," my mother says. "They watch these murder shows on TV and they think of big ugly men with junk food guts and rusty knives stuck through their belts. They hear about maimed hookers and shallow graves. Most people like to believe the worst, especially if it's about something they've never seen up close."

The truckers we've caught rides with have almost always had big laughs and outrageous stories. They tell us about their backroad breakdowns, their close shaves. The crazies and the lonelies and the loons who cross their paths. Stress and booze, and what booze does when folks are stressed. They know all about lunatics, and even more about angels. A few told us about their encounters with wild animals, late at night on quiet rural roads when the moon was too bright—escaped zoo animals, endangered species. Wonderful and terrible, both. Once or twice a trucker described seeing some mythological beast. *Cryptids*, one called them. A man-sized creature with moth wings keeping pace above the treetops. A wolf on two legs loping alongside the road. An ape too big to be human, hurling rocks from the shadowed roadside. Stories that froze my pulse before they made me laugh.

Truckers are soft souls. I don't care what the murder shows say. They keep pictures of their wives and kids taped to the dash, hanging from the rearview. Pretty women and grinning kids forever smiling back at them in sun-bleached colors. We've never once caught a ride with a trucker who didn't share his food, offer a blanket or a jacket. Make a point of switching to a different radio station if we asked, roll the windows up or down as we wanted.

Catching rides with strangers. Way more often than not, those are good times. All the talking, laughing, sharing. The quiet, the caution. The respect that comes in silences. But it can be scary, too. Like when they try to get Momma or me to drink, like when they watch me too close. Often it's both happy and scary, the way it feels having one hand on your throat while another tickles you. You want it to stop, but you're still laughing.

When I was eight or ten, we hitchhiked east and a university student stopped for us. I remember it was east, because we were heading toward the coast. I remember his name was Gabriel, and he drove a beaten-up vintage Golf his grandfather had left him. He wore a black leather jacket, it was scuffed and ripped in places. He was going to visit his girlfriend for a few days.

Girlfriend. The way he had said this word: like it was so sweet and special on his tongue. Like he was so proud to have it in his mouth. Later Momma told me that was because he was in love.

"Love makes men softer, safer," she said. "It changes the things they would and wouldn't do, almost overnight. It changes them a lot. If love isn't real, explain *that.*"

Love. I've heard the word before. Said to me. But I didn't feel any power in it. I guess, I don't know how to do it right yet.

We drove through the night. Momma and Gabriel talking in low, friendly tones, their voices clouded against the hum of the engine, the tics and jumps in the road. When I lay down on the backseat he put his jacket over me. I remember the smell. Young, musty. Hair oil and sweat, aftershave, spice. Boy smells, but not the bad kind that smother the air and make me feel like I'm burning up inside.

There was the old couple we met when I was seven or maybe nine, when we hitchhiked north and they stopped for us. Man and woman, greyed out but kind. They took us all the way up to the mountains, to a border town somewhere before the woods start. They bought us fudge at one of the local stores. *Handmade*, they said. *Best in the world*, they told us. It was. Like burnt honey set into squares, sweet and smooth and so rich I nearly threw up on the drive back out.

We didn't stay in that town very long.

"But why aren't you in school, honey?" the old lady said, turning to look back at me.

"She's home-schooled," my mother said. Her voice rushed and tight in a way it seldom is, because she was trying to shove something confident in there. She sat up, messing with her seatbelt like there was something wrong or uncomfortable in the way it crossed her. Her smile came and went like a light being flicked on and off.

Later I realized she was angry. "Dumb old ducks telling me how to raise my child," she said. "Do you know how many kids would kill to go on road trips all the time?"

How many kids would kill? I don't know.

Heading south, north. To the mountains, away from the sea. Riding high up in trucks with burly drivers who crack rude jokes and complain about their hemorrhoids in ways that make the stories funny.

It's not so bad. It's not so bad at all. Like there's a hand on my throat, but I'm laughing anyway.

"Don't think about it, babe," Momma says. "All we have is now, and now is all that matters."

That hand on my throat. And I'm laughing.

12

ANYWAY.

Susie. The guy with a girl's name. The guy with the clenching hands he hasn't used to touch me yet. Only her. His hands on her hips, her thighs, her breasts. Grasping, clasping. Open and shut.

"You don't care if your kid hears us?" Susie said the first night we crashed over.

"Why should I? She's not a baby. Plus, it's the most natural thing in the world. Like, *literally.*"

Susie watched me watching her.

"Hey, kid," she called to me, turning away from him with her arm slack around his neck. "You don't mind if Susie and me make friends, do you?"

"I thought you already were," I said, spreading my smile so my mother laughed and Susie stared at me. Eyes stuck.

I turned away because I was starting to blush. My heart stepping up like I was about to panic. The eye in my forehead itched. I messed my hair into my eyes and unzipped my bag. Cover. Distraction.

Please stop looking at me.

"Hey, angel," Momma said later that night, sneaking back to me in the total darkness with a towel closed between her breasts. "You don't need to be so scared of your momma's friends. They're your friends, too. Okay?"

Wrapping me up close to her so we fell asleep again.

Friends. As if any of them have been people she knew before. Really, they're just strangers. Really, they're the legal occupants of apartments or houses with clean enough beds and maybe some food in the cupboards. Temporary roommates. Makeshift providers. Even the ones who sort of do become friends shift out of our lives after a while. An overstayed welcome has a way of killing love.

Love makes men softer, safer. If love isn't real, explain that.

I guess it's real enough in the time it lasts. An hour, a day, a week. However long it takes for things to break.

***

Susie is younger than most of our past friends have been. Or if he's not so young, he acts like he is. Kid with a cap and crow's feet. Overpriced sports shoes, chipped coffee mugs. Fancy leather lounge suite. Tin cans for ashtrays. No decent crockery. He spends a lot of time on his phone talking about 'menus' and 'suppliers'. 'Deliveries' and 'grades'. He doesn't wear a suit, he doesn't work set hours. I have a pretty good idea what it is he does for a living, but I won't ask about it outright. I guess Mom must know already, too, so there's no point mentioning it. There's nothing dangerous here so far. He lets me sleep on his couch while Mom shares his bed, and he hasn't tried to sneak up on me or spy on me or anything that I can tell.

I would know, because I always do.

It's in the eyes at first. I'll get up from the table to go fill a glass with water or something, and I'll feel the skin on the back of my neck start to burn. I'll know without looking back that they're staring at me, watching me. Things quiet. The air thickens. I'll get nervous, and it's difficult to move naturally.

My steps lurch, my hands jerk. Friends of ours who get like this, they won't look away until I look at them—and then his fixed gaze shifts, and there'll only be a smirk left on his face. Something knowing. Something smug.

Then anything I say will require a physical response. I say *I'm hungry* or *I'm tired* or *Where's the remote*, it doesn't matter what, anything, and the response will come with a hand on my shoulder. Fingers wrapping over my hip. A pat on the rump with a firm hand that hits a touch too hard, but not so hard I'm allowed to say anything. Occasionally a kiss on the forehead, leaving a too-wet residue slimy on my skin. These are not real signs of love. These are gestures of false affection matched nicely with empty words. They're excuses to come closer.

It only gets worse after that.

I've learned to plug the keyholes in bathroom doors with tissue paper. I've learned to sleep with my jeans on, snug fit all the snugger with a great big belt closed over the button, the shiny metal teeth of the zipper locked tight. If I can find one, I'll use a belt with the kind of buckle so big it clangs when it's pulled loose.

It isn't always enough. When Mom drinks too much or takes too many pills—because this has happened, too—she sleeps on a planet far, far away. No amount of ringing belt buckles will bring her crash-landing back to whatever single-bedroom apartment or quiet suburban duplex we're calling home.

Susie. Girl-named guy with the clenching hands. Grasping, clasping. Open and shut on nothing but air. We're staying at his house, but something about him tells me he's still looking for home. Just like we are. Just like me.

13

THERE'S NOTHING WRONG with keeping some things to yourself. I know. But my mother holds details back like they're black secrets with teeth, or monsters hovering in hidden places. Vicious things that can only come out when you look them in the eye. She leaves a lot of blanks for me to stare at. It's not only about Auntie Clem—all those versions I've been told about how we got to stay with her, and later why we left.

I don't know the name of the place where I was born. I don't know where we were when I took my first steps. I don't know where we lived when I spoke my first word. I'm not even exactly sure how old I am. My mother lies about her age all the time. And if she won't say hers, then I can't know mine.

I know who I am, but I don't always know *what*. I'm a child. I'm a daughter. I'm both. I'm neither.

Usually Mom says I'm twelve, maybe thirteen. People sometimes guess my age at sixteen, but only with the makeup and the clothes. When I wash my face clean late at night, before I crawl into whichever bed I'll get to call mine for the next few hours, I stare at my reflection in whatever bathroom mirror I happen to be standing in front of, and I see skin that's smooth and firm and peach-perfect. I see wide eyes, soft and naked without any hard black lines. I see a nude mouth, and curved cheeks I hope will hollow down at some point. And I ask myself, *How old are you?* I could easily be twelve. Or fifteen. Puberty hit me early and slow, like it was in a hurry to get started but unsure about what exactly it wanted to change. Locking me in a kind of half-state. It's only my face that might betray the truth about how young or how old I truly am.

Make your age work for you, my mother says. What she really means is: *Just lie.*

I'm thirteen. Or I'm fourteen. Some days I look like I'm fifteen, or sixteen. When I'm made-up, I can push for eighteen. But my life is my mother's life and hers is mine, and everything that happens to one of us happens to the other. Life experience doubled up, crushed into moments and gasps of time that would be too big for either of us on our own.

I'm a kid. I'm a teen. I'm neither. I'm both. Sometimes in my head, I'm at least fifty years old.

***

Back in Carris with Auntie Clem, I was as close to a kid as I ever got to be. I didn't know about staying in strangers' homes, how each place has its own smell, its own feel. Some secret, precise blend of detergents and skin cells oiled into the tile, rubbed into the wood. I didn't know about motel rooms, how they always smell like whoever was there before you, even if the carpets are clean and there's no dust on the TV or the windowsills. Even if the sheets are white-bright and fresh and there are no dark marks pressed into them. Cigarette smoke and sweat and dried urine lurk in the corners, catching the edges of the air. Bleach and lemon-scented air freshener barely cover the taint of spilled booze and stomach bile. Back in Carris, I didn't know about highways and bridges that go over the roads, or the way gas stations light up the night, getting brighter and warmer as you walk toward them on aching feet. I didn't know about parks, and the people who go to them.

Some of this is sad, but not all of it.

This is why if anyone asks me outright, I tell them I grew up on a smallholding. I tell them I was home-schooled. I tell them I lived for a while in a different world to most—that I stayed young and got old both at the same time, from being so sheltered, from being so independent, both at once.

It's true the way you can make anything true if you say it the right way.

14

THERE'S NOTHING SPECIAL about Susie, no matter what he wants to think. There's nothing unique about his house, his lifestyle, his stupid Star Wars jokes. Every time, every single one of them, they start to think they're ahead of us. Some in small ways, some enough to make them think they're untouchable—as the owner of our current beds, the master of our daily comforts. This isn't always bad. Being underestimated only gives us more gaps. But if it is bad, it means things are about to shift over. That kind of change, it can't always be stopped.

Susie? There's nothing special about him. He's just another *friend* I've yet to figure out.

These single guys we've known before.

Mr. Big Car, Mr. Nice Shades, Mr. Trimmed Beard.

Julian, Edward, Kyle.

Max, Barney, Sam.

The names they gave or the names we made up for them. Still so much the same.

Unshaved cheeks and musty shirts. Dirty tiles, scattered socks. Dishes piled up in kitchen sinks, Tetrised together, bonded by scum. The smells of slippery armpits, unwashed hair. There was that time when the towels all got hung up outside. Skewered to the fence, hooked on barbed wire. The metal ripped tiny holes in the fabric, but he didn't care. There was the bathroom with an old soap bar by the basin, left there so long it had hardened to something like stone. The kitchen with cupboards all crammed with plastic bags and old beer bottles. Empty glass. The one-bedroom apartment with a shower-bath, no curtains, big windows. So much light in there, I seemed to glow.

Or. And.

Sprinkler systems, paved front drives. A spare car, maybe, something sleek that seldom leaves the garage. Sometimes mom gets the keys for a while.

Or.

Garages with shelves and tools lining each wall. Pet hair. Chewed up armchairs. Dogs—the friendly kind, the yappy kind, the kinds that scare you off. Mostly dogs that make my heart hurt. Wishing I was theirs, and they were mine.

And.

There was the place with a thick, yellow tide mark in the bathtub, never scrubbed. Even after all that bubble bath. Those soapy hands. The same one with the princess bed, trussed up in pink. More ruffled things and ribboned things than I'd ever seen. A little girl's bedroom. A girl not me. And those tongues so thick they filled my mouth, made my jaw crack. Sour and turgid as keel slugs, flexing down my throat. I saw a documentary on them late one night. Keel slugs, not tongues.

And.

Shower drains shining like round metal eyes. White tile glossed, waxed. Glass-top coffee tables, marble counters. Furniture so stiff and squeaky you're almost scared to sit, but it's never so bad with a few cushions, some blankets. Mohair, bamboo weave, something soft like velvet but fluffy like wool. Wrapped around your feet and knotted over your knees.

Blankets like that never smell bad. Cigarette smoke maybe, at most. The guys who live in these kinds of homes are what my mother calls 'yuppies'. She says this with a wink, masking how bad she'd rather roll her eyes. Yuppies? They're not so bad. At least they always smell good. At least their nails are trimmed. Worse are the guys who're divorced, kept their money, live like lone wolves in their polished lairs. There was the place with the fancy coffee machine nobody knew how to work. The one with the swimming pool that came partway indoors. I slipped climbing out, cut open my knee. Blood in the water, blood on the tile. Scarlet on white. Gleaming. The way my mother screamed.

Sean, Andrew, Bernard, Cal.

Mr. Jackson, Mr. Bruce.

McCarrie, London, Hughes.

It wasn't always clear at first what they wanted, not with all of them. If it was my mother, or me. Or something in-between.

***

The first friend I remember close to me like this was Kyle. An investment banker, some kind of broker, something risky involving big numbers that makes at least one kind of man decide he's important. Broad and pot-bellied and recently divorced. Not that any of this mattered. I was nine, maybe ten.

"Don't cause any trouble," he had said, but there was a laugh in his voice, happy and hushed.

Mom had stepped out to return some videotapes. It was that kind of time.

He bent me over the edge of his daughter's bed, my knees on her thick, velvet-touch carpet, my arms out flat on her tangled duvet. I thought he was going to spank me at first—I didn't know why, but I was so used to not knowing why so many things happened this seemed almost okay—but instead he lifted up my dress and pulled down my panties and knelt down behind me. Staring at the parts of me I couldn't see. His breath thick and hot on the backs of my thighs.

That was the first time. It took a few more weeks of this before he started using his fingers—all touch, no push, because 'Your Momma might get mad if I make you bleed, right?'—and then his tongue, but we moved away without him not long after. So who knows what might've happened next.

When I think back on him now, my hidden eye opens and everything around me flashes black and grey. Confusion and panic pound through me, my thoughts fuzz over in a white froth like Coca-Cola poured too fast. Between breaths, I see him on his knees. Strobe images.

Flash.

Blood runs down the side of his head in a dark syrup, closing over his cheek and filling his mouth as he looks up at me. Shock-wide eyes. His pockets are full of Polaroids. They shuffle out and hit the floor like oversized playing cards as he twitches, spasms, jolts around. Automaton unwired.

It's almost as if I try to kill him in these dreams. Hurting him, watching him die. Not because I want him to die. But if he does, I want to watch.

It's different in this town, though. This place with its dusty air that makes me sneeze, its water tower staring down. It doesn't feel so crazy at Susie's house.

At fourteen or maybe fifteen, or even at sixteen or maybe seventeen, I'm still below Susie's interest range. He stares at my mother, not me. Smirking like he wants to leap at her the first chance he gets—only he isn't trying to hide it. He calls her *Doll-Face*. He calls her *Babe*. When he screws her, I swear the whole neighborhood can hear him. This freaks me out a little. Aren't men supposed to be quiet, while the women make all the noise? He's worse than a woman. A barrage of sudden moans and yells and bellows. My mother's cries are whispers compared to his. The whole thing makes me awkward, itchy. Makes me want to bang the door open, or maybe solder it shut—I can't decide which would be better. He's theatrical, he's clownish. He laughs at anything, everything. Next to him, my mother seems much older, but maybe only because he acts so young. Turns her into a parody wannabe of a fresher kind of girl, while he treats her like the rebel youngster she once was, and only sometimes still is.

Look at me, I want to say to him.

Why don't you look at me?

I want to see inside his eyes. Whatever it is he's hiding there.

15

MOMMA'S TOLD ME once or twice—and sometimes I remember—about the doll I had when I was really little. *Samelsa*. A name I made up myself. Mom says I wouldn't stand for it when anyone dared mishear me and try to call her 'Sam'.

"Sam is a girl-name for hookers and strippers. Maybe waitresses," she says. "I think you knew that, too. Even then. If people dared call your doll 'Sam' you'd give them the blackest evil eye. That look on your face! It was like a witchy old woman who'd just caught her neighbor's dog peeing on her front porch."

It makes me giggle, the way she says this. Like I'm a shrunken hag underneath what people see, and they should really be afraid of me.

Samelsa had a plastic face with painted freckles and big blue eyes that stayed stuck open. She was always staring. In my lap or under my arm or under the covers with me, she stared at Momma, she stared at the walls, she stared at the ceiling. When I turned her around and looked at her, she stared at me. I took her everywhere. A part of me remembers as much—the feel of her soft bulk under my arm, pressed against my ribs. Her hair in matted whorls of plastic, coarse and prickly beneath my hand.

"You were so lonely," my mom says. "It took me way too long to figure out you needed friends. I thought the only friend you needed was me. And there you were, playing games and make-believe with a doll that couldn't even talk back. I'm sorry, babe. I was just a kid myself, you know. An angry little girl with a baby she loved but didn't know how to take care of."

I remember holding Samelsa on my lap when Momma and me first started doing puzzles at the kitchen table. Her small, soft body slid off my knees when I jiggled my feet, when I moved around too much. She'd hit the floor and stare up at me with her solid, ever-open eyes. Waiting for me to reach down and take hold of her, pull her close to me again. I remember pressing fresh raspberries to her plastic face—an act of love, of sharing—and my horror when the pink-red taint wouldn't wash off after. Raspberries still make me think of Carris. There was a bush somewhere down by the fence, heavy with caterpillars. They showed up each year in the spring. Tiny, misplaced hairs twitching in the foliage, fatter and fatter as the weeks passed, until some got so heavy they fell off their leaves and smashed themselves on the pavement below. Green mulch and shattered skin-casings sticking to the soles of my shoes. If I stepped on them barefoot, the cold crush of their insides slid up between my toes. So I stopped where I stood and stared down in sick fascination.

I guess Samelsa was with me then, too.

This part I can't say myself, but the way Momma tells it, one day I walked over to the well at the bottom of the slope behind Auntie Clem's house, and threw Samelsa down there. I don't remember doing this at all, but I see her small boneless body falling away from me, vanishing down the black hole. I don't remember it, but I hear the splash.

"I guess she must've done something wrong," Mom says. "For you to toss her away like that."

70

I guess. I didn't ask her, or myself, *What crimes can a doll commit?* I don't ask now either, because why try? The way my mother says things happened isn't always the way I remember them. It gets confusing when I look at the in-between. It gets difficult, because the eye I hide starts to itch like it wants to open, and I don't want my normal eyes closed when I hear the real answers.

Maybe I did it in fury, in a tantrum. Spoiled kids probably do ruin their toys more than normal kids. Maybe I did it to test my own courage. Walking to that circle of stone wall, pulling myself up to the edge on my elbows. Staring into the cold black. Dangling Samelsa over the edge. Knowing how final it would be, letting go.

Maybe I did it just to see if I could.

"It surprised the hell out of me," my mother says. "It scared your Auntie Clem. Shook her up. She didn't want to believe you'd done such a thing. She was so upset over it, I'd swear it was like *she* was the one who'd given you that doll." And she chuckles, but it's a dark sound and she shakes her head.

My momma talks in a voice like sliding, pointed silver when she tells me Samelsa got tossed down the well, and nobody understood why. She holds my hands, she pushes her gaze deep into mine. "I took it as a sign," she says.

A sign for her to interpret. Why did she decide this was a sign for her, when I'm the one who did it? I'm the one who committed the crime. Not her, not my doll. I'm the one who took something helpless, something I loved, and threw it away into darkness.

"All mothers make mistakes," my momma says. "Even a baby doll-mother like you were then. Every mistake a mother makes is a solution that turned out wrong. Thinking back on you throwing your doll away, it was one of the things that helped me decide we needed to get out of Carris. The place was so small and so isolated we were both half-crazy. I knew no matter how strange or scary a future alone might seem, I had to try and do what was best. I had to figure out what that was."

"But I loved my doll." It's a fact I feel, even if it isn't one I really know.

"Maybe you did, babe," my mother says. "And maybe you didn't. You can't always trust your memories." She holds her index finger up as she speaks, fat and curled as a caterpillar. Twitching between words. "Especially childhood memories. Your imagination is so big and so bold when you're young, you don't always know the difference between dreams and facts. I remember how it is. How the things you dream up can seem so real." My mother's silver smile softens. She moves her gaze away from mine. She lowers her hand. She says, "Remembering things wrong can get people into trouble for no reason at all. You don't want that on your head. Believe me."

I know this is true. I also know there are lots of different parts of trouble hidden around in so many separate pieces of the truth.

"Trust me," she says. "Be careful what you remember. Be careful what you say you remember." What she means is, *Be careful about saying what you think you know.*

What Momma doesn't say, but what we both know: I never needed that doll anyway. My mother is the closest thing I'll ever have to a sister. She's the best friend I'll ever know. If blood is thicker than water, then together the two of us make blood and water both equally thick. We make it something liquid and viscous and shining, a bonding of the essence, shifting between her and me. So much more important than thread and stuffing and glass eyes, wrapped in a half-torn dress.

DOLL CRIMES

***

I still feel bad about that doll. The one I saved from a hooker name. A doll I carried around with me for years, and now remember only in flashes. Bare, bright impressions, like seeing something through burned retinas. Seared over everything in a glowing silhouette.

The same as Loki.

I barely met Loki, but when I remember him it's with a sick stirring so deep and violent it's like there's a clawed hand rammed down my throat. Churning my guts around. Turning my insides into so much fine flesh confetti.

I remember Uncle Steve and his puppies. The ice tea in the milkshake glass. Those sounds, the click and purr the camera made. And that other kind of light, flashing in my eyes.

16

"**H**EY, WE DON'T have to go home if you don't want to."

Home.

We're standing outside the train station in the late afternoon, the business rush and crush around us, overdressed people in uncomfortable shoes making queues and talking on phones and shouldering each other out the way. We stand to the side and watch the chaos. High above and over everyone's heads, the notice boards switch information in neat, color-coded lines.

Arrived.

Departed.

Delayed.

Names of places I know and places I don't. Wherever we go, or go back to, it'll never be the same.

"Yeah, I know, Mom," I say, staring up.

"It's just, the thing is . . . "

The way she won't finish the thought, I know what she's about to say.

"I was so sure we'd be heading back with some cash today, I didn't—you know—"

"You didn't take any extra?" It sounds like a question, but it shouldn't be.

She shrugs at me, guilty eyes. "We can try to sneak through?"

We've done this before, but it's easier in subway systems. Train stations check tickets better. They've got people or machines, or both. It's not so easy getting in, and it can be even harder getting out. At a subway station, lots of strangers will want to help. Young guys usually, the types in dirty jeans and battered shoes, headphones roped around their necks in spaghetti cords. He'll let you cuddle up close to his back. Shuffle his feet with yours as the stile turns. Laugh with you on the other side. Nod, or smile.

"Fuck the Illuminati," one guy said when we stepped clear, and gave me a high-five. Grinning like we'd pulled off a heist or blown up a bank. Stuff like that is always fun. Even though I'd never heard of the Illuminati before.

But we're not in a subway station.

"If we have to, I guess . . . "

"Hang here a while," she says. "I'm gonna find the bathrooms."

"But—"

She shifts the strap on her bag and turns into the crowd. Slim shoulders, sleek hair. Liquid steps. In the time I take to hesitate, she vanishes too deep into the thick and I'm nervous and edgy on my feet. It's too late to follow. I drop my bag down to my hand, resting it on my foot by the strap. I shuffle back a few steps so I can lean against a pillar. Wide column with people littered all the way around.

Automatons. Buzzing back and forth.

She better be able to find me again.

The people near me are all stuck in some chore. Digging something out, putting something away. Talking on the phone—so many people are doing stuff on their phones. I've never had my own phone. I'm not allowed to touch my mother's. Not even now, when I'm as good as grown-up. I think.

The clock reads 17:12.

Two girls—around my age—shuffle up a few steps from me, sharing a magazine between them. They pop gum and point at pictures. They're talking like it's something serious, but I can't hear them over the echoes and chaos of rush-hour sounds. One of them says something she thinks is funny—I can tell by the way she grins as she speaks. The other cracks a smile. Half-mouthed.

A young, executive-type guy in a plum-colored shirt, open tie, looks me up and down as he passes, turning his head to catch my gaze over his shoulder. My eyes freeze on him as the third one twitches open. I catch it shut, slamming down an image of him stumbling forward as he grabs at his throat—something black sluicing from his mouth, running over his hands. Hot as tar. Smoking where it spreads. There's panic in his eyes. Like he doesn't know why.

He's gone when I see clear again. Another stranger I killed for no reason.

I'm craving chocolate. Something smooth I can bite all the way into before it melts. A flood rich as blood. Is blood sweet? I don't know.

The clock reads 17:22.

"Hey, babe. *Hey*," my mother says. She comes from nowhere—from around the other side of the pillar, at my shoulder quicker than I can turn. I face her and she's flushed, breathing the way she does when she's trying to cool down. She's always edgy when it happens like this. "You've got two envelopes, right?"

"Yeah."

"Gimme."

I dig into my back pocket and hand them to her.

She sighs. "They're *bent*."

"It's not too bad."

She sighs again, checking them over. She takes the one that looks smoother, and hands the other back. "Okay. Best we got. Give me ten minutes, angel. Ten."

I jam the envelope back down my jeans.

The clock reads 17:24.

I watch where she's headed. There's a man at one of the ATMs against the far wall. He's counting the money he's withdrawn, a slim pile poised at the open lips of his wallet. His thick fingers crawling delicately through the folds.

How did I murder plum-shirt guy, and not see this one? I know his type just by looking at him. The eyes blurred behind dirty glasses, the thinning hair. Creased shirt, cracked belt. The type who washes his face but not his neck, his palms but not the backs of his hands. Fresh soap and old sweat. He'd taste musty, bitter, old. Leaving that taint in my hair, around my throat.

My mom walks up to him. She greets him with an easy smile. As if she's met him somewhere before. He flinches like she might lunge at him. Bite him. It lasts only a second, but it's there. My mother steps closer and sweeps her arm out straight to point me out. I cross one foot behind the other, clasp my hands behind my back. I stretch my smile. When he looks at me, I wave.

Little girl pose.

He stands, staring.

The envelope and cash switch from hand to hand. It's clumsy, because he's not looking down. He fumbles his wallet, then the envelope. He remembers himself, catching both back and shoving his wallet into his pocket before it can fall again. He rolls the envelope into a stiff curve, unsure where to put it. The pictures will be even more bent now.

My mother moves like she wants to hug him, but he steps away. It's probably been a long time since he was touched. There's something in his face, but I can't read it. Like he wants to vomit, like he wants to run. Like a light just went on inside.

I'd eat it alive.

I'd eat it alive.

It's always this way with the guys who hang out in public areas. A twist under their skin, dark adrenalin rushing their veins. Filthy as ditch water, murky as their eyes. They're looking for something, but when they get it they don't know what they wanted to do with it, or why. Sometimes it's fake—that consternation, that fear—but sometimes it's not.

There's the City Library up in the capital. Coded knocks on bathroom stalls. Those scenic spots along the highways where people like to stop. Parks.

There was the guy who followed us after, shadowing our route home. We didn't realize for an hour. Zigzagging back, making a frightened crisscross through buses and platforms and thinning streets. My third eye wide open, something stuck screaming in my throat so I couldn't make a sound. My mother's face too white, her eyes too wide.

There was the man who wanted me to meet him in the bathrooms, who threatened to make a scene when my mother said no. She saw the color rising in his face and she snatched the envelope back. She did her shoulder-turn, her fast-walk away from him and toward me. Catching me hard and urgent with her eyes. We headed straight out the station. The metal-panic taste of blood and adrenalin thick in our saliva. Lights in our eyes set to spinning in crazy, urgent red.

Flash.

Those pulses, those bursts.

We've never gone back.

The clock reads 17:26.

I'm hungry. I've lost track of my mother. She's somewhere, not far.

I hope she can find me again.

The clock reads 17:34.

Some oblivious old guy with a travel case on wheels stands around, blocking the view ahead of me. His mouth hangs open, eyes wide and blank. He's looking around, confused.

Catching flies.

I don't get how so many people in the world forget to close their mouths.

"There you are, Houdini," my mother says. She appears at my side again, jostling past the open-mouthed automaton. "Where did *you* go?"

"Where did *I* go? Where did *you* go?"

She giggles and grabs my shoulders. "I know, I know. I zipped into the ladies to take a pee and have a quick look." She taps on her feet. "He gave us something like three times more than I asked. Like he just shoved it all at me. We're *rich*."

We're rich about as often as we're poor, which means this is always nice to hear. If it lasts a day. A week. A few weeks. What does she say? *Believe in love anyway.*

"I want pizza rolls," I tell her.

"Pizza rolls? Nah . . . think bigger."

But I like pizza rolls.

"I dunno? *Lobster* then?"

"Nuh-uh," she wrinkles her nose. "Remember that time we tried it? That port town a year back? *Way* overrated for those prices."

I don't remember the lobster. But maybe I thought it was crab.

"How about we get something from a nice restaurant, and bring it back to share with Susie?"

She laughs like the idea is stupid. "Susie makes his own money, babe. This is for *us*."

"Seafood, though?"

I'd be scared if I ever met a live lobster, face-to-face. Hard shell and serrated pincers. No nerves on his surface so I can hurt him back.

"No," she says. "I'm not in the mood for that, either."

I want a roast beef sandwich and a plate of apple strudel piled with cream. I want garlic bread and ratatouille, chocolate mousse. I want all the things we never get to eat.

"How about a nice big eisbein?" she says.

Elite bar food. Big knuckle bone wrapped in a mass of pink flesh. There's something that I heard somewhere. In a nightmare, in a dream. Maybe a detail in a magazine article, something horrible in the news. *Human flesh tastes like pork.*

We're pushing back toward the exits. The people thin out in this direction, knots and stragglers vanishing behind us in bursts of dust.

Automatons.

Dust storms.

I won't look over my shoulder. I don't want to. My dark eye stutters open and shut.

We probably won't be home till after dark, now. She'll probably drink some wine.

We don't have to go home, she said.

I don't want to go.

Home.

17

MY MOTHER WOULD hate hearing this, but she wasn't the only one who got hurt back in Carris. She wasn't the only one who had stuff to cry over. I knew that same fist-round-the-ears feeling, the same helpless fear of a mismatched fight. Powerless. My mother's unravelings were sporadic, sharp. Her mind a drawstring bag with a snapped cord, contents sliding out the mouth, slipping loose across the floor. A storm of tiny, shattered marbles.

Funny how when she was hurting me, she thought she was the one really hurting.

Those moments got closer together in the weeks before we left. She would hate hearing this, but they're the reason I feel the same when she says we had to leave Carris.

Not because of Clem, Momma. Because of you.

I don't remember where I was when I first recalled this, but I feel the sun beating down on me, tightening my damp skin. My hair is wet and whatever I'm wearing clings across my breasts, between my legs. My eyes are shut so I only see red. I'm not sure on all the details, but my mind fills in the gaps.

Clem had been gone about a week, and Momma was getting itchy and restless the way she always was when we were stuck out there together, just the two of us, for too long.

Knowing Clem would be home soon. That suddenly it was too soon—the house in dust and chaos and secret spills. Like a backroom gambling den. Bottles lined along the floors, pee stains behind the TV. The fridge cleared out, buzzing on a crumb-scarred stick of butter. A tub of yoghurt with a new white film gliding over its sharp-smelling surface. The floors were tacky-sticky, the bedsheets smelled like night sweat. Our laundry lay crammed around the washing machine, spilled across the floor. No three neat piles on top the way we usually did it: *Clean, Can-Wear-Again, Wash*. All the dirty mixed in with the fresh.

"It's today or tomorrow," Momma was saying. To herself, not me. "Even if it is tomorrow, be ready for today."

The phone hadn't rung in days. There was nothing written down. Asking my mother when Auntie Clem was coming home, the answer was always 'Soon'. Said a touch sharper each time.

"Soon."

And she gave me a damp cloth to run over the tables. Left me to make pretty patterns on wood with sweeps of moisture. Arcs and butterflies and loops, glossy on scarred wood.

I don't recall where I was when I remembered this, but it made the back of my head sting.

"Not everything is a fucking *game*," my mother said. She pulled the cloth back out my hand, rubbing the table down so hard she chipped a nail. She threw the cloth back at the kitchen sink, breathing hard like her feelings were frothing over and she didn't have enough space in her chest. She got out the wine. The kind that comes in a box and has pictures of grapes on the front. It always tasted too sour to me, burning my throat before it burned my eyes. It isn't grape juice, even if it looks like it. My mother drank a lot more when it was the two of us alone.

"Today or tomorrow," she said, and her eyes ambled over to me.

Auntie Clem. I wanted her then.

"When did we last wash your hair?"

I'm not clear on what was happening when this memory came back to me, but my bathing suit straps are sliding off my shoulders, gathering across my chest where my cleavage starts. Edging down, careful and slow, catching on my nipples. There are hands sliding up between my thighs, ready to close in. Clench. I'm not sure if they're someone else's hands, or mine.

We had to wash my hair.

Had to, she said.

Gush of boiling water. My ponytail untied, my dress pulled off over my head. My mother put her glass down on the side of the bath. Steam billowed up to the ceiling in thick drifts. It was hard to see anything in the small, closed-in room. Clouds of heat. The mist that sweats.

"Get in," she said. Using her mad-mommy-voice, the one I liked the least. The one she pitched too high, her eyes tainting dark. "Come on, girl. I said." Grabbing my arm and pulling me to the side. "Get. In."

I said.

She glared at me through strings of greasy hair, those loose strands clumped together. She smelled like sweat and she smelled like wine and her hands shook.

When did we last wash your hair? she said to me.

"It's hot, Momma."

"Hot is *good.* Hot is *clean.* Hot burns all the bad stuff off. Now *get in.*"

The surface of the water smoked and rippled. The tap gushed like thunder.

"Turn it off first, please, Momma."

She yanked the tap shut. She sighed. "Help me out here, babe." From the way her eyebrows were pushed close together, her head was starting to hurt. From the way her hands were trembling, she needed to eat.

I know this now. I didn't know it then.

I looked back at the bathtub. A snapshot vision I've saved in my mind and set to motion—the picture of that smoking surface, the way it rolled around the edges. Choppy ripples, riding the rim.

"No."

I can't recall who was with me when I pulled this day back, but there's a heart beating against my ear. There are hands in my hair, an arm closed around my shoulders. It's heavy, strong. I'm warm and I'm sweating. Hot but I'm shivering. Stiffening my muscles to mask the quaking under my skin. And I think I like this, but I'm worried I might not. I want to like it, but I'm afraid I don't.

That day.

My mother's hands closed around my waist in a sudden clamp. Her grip tightened as she lifted me, hoisting me over the walled edge of the bathtub. It passed beneath me like a hard, white smile. Steam stung at my feet, the backs of my thighs. Tiny needle tips of heat scattered across my body. It was only a second, a split second. Her hands and her nails dug into my skin in tiny, biting arcs. The water closed over the balls of my feet and shattered up my back, ripped across my buttocks. My scream was so loud it was like a pig squeal, even to me. I kicked, sending a sharp spray back over my mother. She shrieked and backed away.

"Shit. *Shit.*" she said. Even saying it so fast, it was still all slurred.

I clambered over the wall of the bathtub, slithering over it and falling back onto the soaked bathmat. My crying eased to heavy sobs as my skin reddened and darkened to a solid scarlet. Watermark shapes flared red against pale.

"Sorry, baby," she said. "Sorry, baby. My baby girl." She was crying with me, her hands hovering over me, desperate to touch but scared. She reached back for the towel and closed it around me in a hug. Her body quaked against mine.

The times my momma hurt me, it was never a thing she wanted or planned. That day in the bathroom, she shivered all the way into her core. Her mouth was pulled tight like she was trying not to scream inside. I breathed her in. Her special *Momma* scent, present always, even when masked with sweat and booze and the fluids that moved between her legs. Those smells she carried around back then. Comforting to me, even when they shouldn't be.

I don't remember what I was doing when I filled in these long-ago details, but I'm staring at my hands. My fingernails. They've been painted creamy nude, soft scarlet and glitter-blue, alternating finger to finger. My ring finger, glitter-blue, has already chipped. I don't remember why, but looking at it makes me sad. The one imperfect thing, ruining everything.

If only that had never happened.

"Come on, baby, let me give you some of this. You'll feel better."

We were in the kitchen. I was still wrapped in the towel. My mother reached across the table for the half-empty bottle, splashing some into a mug where it mixed with her cold coffee.

"Come on, babe, just a few sips."

The liquid was warm and bitter as vinegar, murky-dark from the coffee and milk. I drank it anyway because my mouth was dry and my throat was thick and I needed something to swallow, no matter how bad the taste.

It took her longer than me to stop crying, even when she

put me straight into bed, damp-haired and naked. Her cheeks shone with salt, stretching tight when she smiled.

"Lie still for a while," she said.

It wasn't near bedtime. It was broadest day. The sun seared across my sheets. She lay down beside me, both of us heavy and tired from crying. Her arms over me, her mouth pressed to the back of my head.

"Clem would kill me," she said. "I wasn't thinking, babe. I don't know why, but I didn't think. You understand, though, don't you? Your Momma isn't perfect, kid. It was just a mistake."

Auntie Clem came back the next day, sometime around dawn. The house still half a mess, those empty boxes of wine left out on the counter. The kitchen floor still tacky-sticky, even though the others were smooth and most surfaces shone. It was a mess frozen at half-cleaned. Stopped at midway point. The worst of how it was still obvious in what was missed.

My momma and me were on the bed together when Clem came in, me still tangled up in my towel, my mother wrapped around me. Legs, arms, skin. Damp sheets and wet floors and blankets dark with stains.

I wish I'd known to pretend nothing had happened. Being a kid makes you stupid. You don't know what foresight is. You betray the ones you love to express your own selfish world.

I don't recall where I was when I remembered this. Someplace that hurt. I guess it doesn't matter now.

Auntie Clem watching Mom wash me at the bathroom sink. Tepid water and a soapy rag.

"It's a phase she's going through," Momma said to her. "This . . . not liking *baths* . . . thing."

"Is that so." It should've been a question, but it wasn't.

"You're just mad because you can't always control things," Mom said.

"You would be a mess if I didn't. *Apparently.*"

I stood at the bathroom sink, and the dry bathtub stared at me. Rust-spotted taps, broken metal chain. My bare skin. My mother wrapped a towel around me.

"Quit staring at her like that, Clem. It's creepy."

"The next time I'm gone, I better not come back to find any new marks on her."

"I'm not my father."

"Then don't be."

18

MY MOM AND me are both asleep on Susie's surprisingly clean queen-size when he gets back from work. We're stripped down to panties and t-shirts, and it's okay, I think, because so far I don't see the need to sleep with jeans on in Susie's house. And I've always loved to sleep close to my mother when I can. Her scent is different when she sleeps, something spicy in the warmth of her sweat. She holds me closer, too. I bury my face in her throat and she locks her elbows through my arms, and the only thing that'll wake us is the pins and needles in our hands and fingers when our stopped blood rushes free.

I'm lying with her in the darkness when I hear his key in the lock, the door squeak open, the scuffle of his feet, the door slam shut. Footsteps.

The room darkens a touch.

"Well, isn't this nice," he says in a loud voice, in a tone that pretends this isn't *nice* at all. "Where am *I* supposed to sleep?"

I'm used to this kind of stupid question. It's posed like it's something innocent, something genuine or fun, but really it's a way to politely bash down a door that shouldn't be opened. A harmless, kind of *why not* innocence thick in the tone. Underneath, there's nothing innocent there at all. But Momma and me know, when we hear this Barney the Dinosaur bullshit, to pretend we believe the words are genuine. Everyone's pretending something. Always. Anyways.

I shift up, sit up, and stare at him across the shadowed room. His arms are at his sides, but braced. Fingers twitching. He stands in silhouette with the hall light on behind him. I can't see his face or read his eyes or his mouth, or his frown. I can't see if he's smiling. But I think I hear a smile in his voice.

"It's okay, Susie." My voice is rusty and slow. I wasn't all the way asleep when he came home, but I was close. "I'll move now."

He doesn't shift, or answer. The only way I know time hasn't stopped in my head, leaving me frozen and dumb again, is from the way he sways. Just a little. The outline of his head, his ears, weaving left and right. Like a cobra in a basket, waiting to be charmed. He's drunk or high or both. I'm small and weak and tired. The nerves in my hands and lips hum, fuzzy and thick. It's the way TV static might feel if it moved against your skin.

I shift away from my mother, slowly so I don't wake her. The bed stutters as I stand. It's hard to stand. My body feels heavy, almost limp. I stumble as I step away, raising my hands to brush my hair out my face as I move. Too much at once, this rush of movement stirring my blood. I stumble like I might fall. Susie takes a step forward. To catch me, I think.

"I'm okay, I'm okay," I mumble.

Behind me, my mother moans in her sleep, like her dream is turning into something she didn't expect. Like a nightmare might be coming.

I step back again and reach for the doorway. Susie stops me with a touch to my elbow. I sway, stand.

"Are you high?" he whispers to me.

I shake my head. "Are you?"

"Yes." He smiles in the hushed light. His eyes are very

bright. "Kind of, I think. But I'm . . . I'm gonna sleep it off now. And then I think we need to talk."

"Talk?"

"Yeah. Talk."

My legs are trembling. All I want is to sit down, or lie down. Even the floor would be fine.

"Is your mom's name really Sheba Cordelia Anna Ruth Hayes?"

I shake my head. "No."

"What's her name?"

I take a moment. I think. "Mom," I say. "Her name is Mom. Sometimes Momma. Sometimes it's even Mother."

He takes in air like he's about to say something, then presses his lips shut tight for a moment. Swallowing those words. "We need to talk," he says again.

I nod. I push past him and he doesn't stop me, though I maybe expected him to. I stumble across the hall and into the living room. The couch is soft and wide, covered in crumpled serviettes and discarded food wrappers. Crumbs, too. Stretching out on it, everything scratches against my skin. The smell trapped in the cushions is dense and stale, thick with something foul.

After a few minutes I get up again, dig through my bags in the dark and pull out a pair of jeans. I slide them on, zip the crotch and collapse back onto the couch.

It's not that I think I really need to wear jeans when I sleep here tonight. Only that the air just got a little cold.

19

TAKE A THICK black marker and draw a line. Before Carris, after Carris. Hold the pen in place too long and watch the ink spread into a wide, bleeding dot. The point of hesitation before we launched off the edge.

Those final days.

I didn't know my mother and Clem weren't friends enough for me. This word Clem chose for me: *Lonely*. When Clem was gone, I didn't know I wasn't friend enough for my mother. The word my mother chose for herself: *Isolated*.

When Clem was away, my mom and me spent our evenings and hours of our nights together, curled up with popcorn and salted crackers, watching dumb TV shows. We still do this now when we can, but it was different then because the house in Carris was home. Not 'we can be anywhere we want to be' home, but the home where our pillows smelled like our hair, there wasn't a room that didn't have signs of us in it, and we all knew the exact right way to jimmy the back door handle so it wouldn't stick. My mom and me ate toffee eclairs and laughed at Bill Cosby. We swapped our pillows around and dug a perfect hollow for us at the end of the couch. I still see the blanket we shared those nights—fluffy, thick, a smoke-swirl of pale and dark blue. We used to fall

beard. How they'd stretch and how they'd smile, lying out on the lawn in shorts and t-shirts, drinking wine coolers and eating oranges. Almost impossible to picture, except for in spare moments toward the end when one of them said something funny. Even then their smiles were like molded rubber, the laughter tuned like piano keys.

People look and act a lot different when they're in suits. Untouched, untouchable. Posed. Sometimes it's like they're hardly human until it all comes off.

My mother was starting to look different like that. Neat hair and clean t-shirts. Painting her nails red, navy blue, baby pink. Changing her shirts the moment they got messed up.

She took a long time getting things from neighbors, down at the gate. Longer than the evening news, and sometimes as much as halfway through the movie after.

All our neighbors, all our friends.

My mother.

Take a thick black marker and draw a line. Press down harder at the end, so the ink bleeds out and leaves a wider mark. That point of hesitation before we launched off the edge.

***

Look, I hardly remember the woman.

I mean, maybe I never knew her at all.

Clem.

Wide shoulders, short hair. The tattoo on her arm, so faded out under stretched skin it was hard to tell what type of bird it was supposed to be. A heron, a hawk, something with wide wings and a curved beak set in loops and circles. Her thick fingers rubbing into my ribcage when she tickled me. It hurt, but had me laughing.

It can be that way sometimes.

I remember the strength around her; the solid, easy feel

94

of safety she brought with her. She picked me up like I was nothing, hoisted high and held tight in her arms.

"Little girl," she called me. "Angel-kid."

I knew she had a way with my mother. A way that pulled my mother close, but also scared her. The way Clem cut her short just by meeting her eyes, twisting her mouth flat and slanted to the side. The way she wasn't scared to yell back when my mother started screaming. Raging in return at her, thick hands clenched to small, round fists at her sides.

Anger is frightening. Like rabid dogs unleashed within, snarling and snapping their crazed way out.

That's what I remember. If I know anything about this at all.

20

I DON'T WANT to *talk* to Susie. What do Susie and me have to *talk* about, anyway?

It's morning again. Day again. At least for now we're 'rich'. I wonder if he even knows. About our money, I mean.

I brush my teeth, I wash my face, I comb my hair out with my fingers. I dig through my mother's shoulder-bag—the denim one with the hole in its lining—and scratch out her lipstick. The dark mulberry one she says is too old for me. I paint my mouth the way she does—watching the lines, following the dips and slopes. I leave my eyes naked.

I'm this girl, I tell myself when I look again at my full reflection. If I had my way, this is the only makeup I'd ever wear. Enough me and enough not-me. The dark shade brightening my skin, lighting up my irises. My face nude but not unmarked. A child with a woman's mouth. Only my eyes are entirely my own.

I pull on my boots and grab my jacket. I ease the front door shut behind me so the deadbolt clicks home instead of snaps.

Out on the town's high street, the morning is frosty and chill and busy. People in suits and smart shirts hurry along the sidewalks with their heads down, backpacks slung over their shoulders, heading towards bus stops or the train station or some destination just around the corner. Each of them—even the business guys in the more formal suits—has something on them or about them that marks them out. A flash of self in a sea of sameness. A SpongeBob Squarepants keychain hanging out a pocket. A Slipknot patch stitched into the side of a backpack. Headphones dangling from their ears, playing something or only pretending to, I don't know. Sometimes I glimpse a jazzy-looking tie as the wind peels back a jacket. I catch a flash of brightly-colored socks as someone steps. Some people wear sunglasses. I would love a pair of sunglasses. A total, muted mask. You can look at anything for as long as you want and nobody can tell what you're thinking.

It's a cold morning but the glare is bright on the pale concrete, flashing off shop windows, steel pipes. My eyes stream like I'm crying, but I'm not.

They each have these pieces of identity, these people, these strangers. But they don't look at each other, or at me. Like they want others to see but not acknowledge. Like what they're carrying with them or on them, it's something only for them.

I can't be jealous about this, because it doesn't matter anyway. They don't matter. When they vanish down the steps to the subway. When they step up onto a bus. When they open some door and push their way inside. They cease to exist right after. Keychains and band patches and all. Them and everything about 'them' vanishes in clouds of dust behind my back. When they round the corner out of my view, they dissipate like tiny golden storms, shattering into the air.

They are not real. They are not here. Not really.

I keep my own head down and my hands hidden in my pockets. I don't look at anyone unless it's out the corner of my eye. I'm not one of them. I'm not a part of them. Nothing I say or do will be remembered by them. Not them—the impermanent people. They vanish down stairs and through doorways as though they never were, and I stay right here.

It's an interesting thought. Sometimes I even make myself believe it for a while.

The coffee shop has a bell over the entrance. It rings as I push the door open—*sharp, metallic*—and I freeze for an instant. The warmth hits my face. Steam, people, bodies, haze. It's darker in here. Shapes bloom then fade in front of my eyes—the steps, the doorway, the sun shining off the outer glass.

The door bumps open again against my back and the cold from outside bites my bare neck.

"Sorry, girl," a voice says over my shoulder as a man pushes past me, for a moment his hand closing on my sleeve.

Sorry, girl.

It takes me a moment to decide if he apologized after or before he touched me.

I don't have money, but I get in the queue and order a coffee anyway. A latte that will come in a tall disposable cup with a plastic lid on it. Inside it'll be rich foam and brown sugar, with cinnamon dusting the top.

At the till I dig through my pockets. I look distressed.

"I—I think it's gone," I say. "My wallet, it's—"

I have to hold the queue up for a full eight minutes before anyone offers to pay for me. Maybe it's the lipstick. I don't look innocent enough.

"What game is this, kid?" the guy at the till says. He doesn't sound angry so much as he does stretched. He's chubby with pitted skin—bad acne when he was younger, has to be. Which means he probably got ignored a lot, or maybe pushed around a lot. Now he has too many wrinkles in his forehead for his age.

See, it all adds up.

"It's just—I had money on me," I say, and my throat swells. My eyes burn and my vision blurs. I guess I'm crying, though I didn't plan to.

"Okay, honey, okay," a woman behind me says. She reaches into her bag and unclips a sleek red wallet—smooth, expensive leather with a golden zip. She hands the cash over to the sad soul at the till and he shakes his head at her as he takes it, but he doesn't say anything. At least there's that.

I take my coffee and I'm still crying, and suddenly I don't want it anymore. This tall plastic thing, hot and waxy. This thing that made me cry.

"It was *in my backpack*," I say as the woman corrals me away from the queue, her arm clasped around my shoulders. I lean into her—habit, I guess—and I feel her stiffen under her silk blouse at my touch, my closeness. I don't know why she should flinch. I washed my hair. I'm sure I smell good. Good enough, anyway.

"You're not carrying a backpack."

"I must've forgotten it at home . . . "

"Well . . . don't you need it for school or something? And aren't you going to be late?"

Sometimes when you don't know the answers to questions, it's better to ignore them when they're asked.

"I can't believe I actually left without it," I tell her. "I *never* leave without it. I didn't even realize . . . "

Her lips thin out. I'm not saying the right things, because now she's shifting over. Some people, when they do something nice it makes them feel nice too. They beam like they're golden inside, and you can tell it's real because they don't think to question you. It doesn't occur to them; they're too blinded by the moment. Other people let it go sour—they ride a wave where all they think about is how wonderful they are. How kind. Like it's not so much about doing something nice, but more about getting to be the hero. This lady here, she's hovering somewhere between the two. I'm not sure where to look. Into her eyes or down at her feet.

"Are you going back home now?" she says. "Or school?"

I don't have a home. Or a school. But I can't tell her that.

"Th—thanks so much," I say. "Only great people do great things."

This phrase never fails when my mother says it. Maybe it sounds better coming out of her mouth. She can pitch it right so it doesn't seem out of place, or condescending, or overdone, or anything bad at all. Saying it now by myself, even I hear how stiff and practiced it is. How insincere.

I turn and push my back toward the doors, brushing against people much taller than me who hide me with their shoulders. I want to be on the street again, away from people who will look me in the eyes, say things to me. See me. No walls in my way, no doors to signal when I walk in or when I try to leave.

My mother made a rule a long time ago that I'm not allowed outside on the streets alone on weekdays, during school hours. I thought I looked old enough today. Enough like *me* for it to be okay.

The woman in the coffee shop—I hope she forgets me soon. I hope she bursts into a mist of fine golden dust, and drifts to nothing in the air behind me.

It's colder outside, but it's brighter too.

21

FROM THE DAY we left Carris and started moving around, in every place we went and in every area we stayed, there would be a park nearby. Some of these parks had ponds, some of them had swing sets and jungle gyms. Some had ice-cream stands and hot dog stalls and small wooded enclaves interspersed with picnic tables. Sections bright under sunshine, others dark from shade.

"We need to stay close to places where you can still go do things outside," my mother said. "Play and stuff. What's a childhood without any trees."

What's a childhood without any trees.

The way she said this, it wasn't a question. I knew she was feeling bad for me, thinking about how big the Carris house was compared to these places we were living now. Swapping all our open space for strange buildings and zigzagging streets. Looking out at a horizon of jagged roofs, and not the Carris hills that rolled around town and rippled in a soft, gliding ascent toward the mountains. Following the signs to train stations, coach depots, platforms and numbered stops instead of walking the front drive from the house down to the gate— the furthest I'd ever gone on foot until we left. None of the new things around me matched the things I'd known before, muting all the reference points and memories that told me what a thing was supposed to look like, how something was supposed to be. Carris flickered through my mind in still images, distant and alien with this new context of what *was*, and how it's no longer what *is*. Images like the view from my window. The long gravel drive walled with old trees and wild bushes. The weeds around the well. None of the parks my mother now took me to matched the pictures appearing then vanishing behind my mind's eye.

I've heard people talk about how they think country kids grow up lucky. I think city kids grow up lucky in another way. The bigger a place is the smaller the things in it seem to get. Dense cities mean shrunken homes: everything trimmed off or cut short or utilized to the inch. Kitchens adjoining with leisure space. Bathrooms the size of parking bays. Swimming pools not much bigger than ponds, and the water sometimes just as murky. In some apartment buildings, the neighbors are so close, you can hear them talking through the walls, and if you climb a tree outside, some old lady will bang on her window and yell at you. City kids learn more about rules, and country kids don't know as many walls.

What's a childhood without any trees.

We'd put our shoes on and unbolt the doors we'd have to lock again behind us. Deadbolts, combinations, chains, sliding metal gates that locked when they slammed. I'd never seen doors with so much armor: each entrance a hard-won exit. We stepped out of whatever living space we'd claimed, headed down a stairwell or across a courtyard, out through a garage or past a reception desk. We walked down this new street or through that back-alley, hand-in-hand like any mother out with her child on a sunny afternoon. Casual shoes and hair tied up off our shoulders. Carrying nothing but a backpack to hold our water bottles and keys, something with sleeves in case it got cold, a change of underwear for in case one of us got messy. Those thick, square envelopes jammed down our jeans pockets.

Some of the parks my mother took me to—the kinds with parking lots and entrance fees and young, peppy staff members who walked around in colorful t-shirts—had cordoned off petting-zoos where they kept small animals for the kids to feed. Friendly things that knew not to bite, pushing their noses through the chain-link fencing, the wooden slats. Sniffing at small, half-open hands with their velvet snouts. Sucking in and puffing out. Nostrils flaring into tiny black holes.

Back in those early days, when we went to a park, Momma did me up in t-shirts, elastic-waist pants. Never skirts or dresses because, *You don't wear those when you're gonna be out in the dirt.* Never makeup because, *You're too young for that, kid.* But she'd give me her lip gloss if I kept asking. Slick, scented oil greasy round my mouth—I licked it off as soon as it was on, no matter how hard I tried to stop myself. Sweet, strawberry tinge. It looked so pretty on my momma, softest pink sheen gliding dots of light back and forth across her lips when she spoke, when she smiled, when she turned her head. For as long as I could keep my tongue off it, it looked pretty on me, too.

We'd walk if the park was close by, catch the bus if it was farther. A different place every week, rolling on a roster. In quiet times, when the bus wasn't too full, Momma took the seat behind me so she could put my hair up in a French braid. Separating it into a dozen smooth, straight sections, piece by patient piece. Undoing and redoing each fine weave until she had it just right. Those tight knots sat close against my skull, secured in looping patterns that gave me headaches that stretched out from my temples, long and taut. Like a rubber band noosed around my skull. But the braids kept any stray strands from slipping loose, falling free. From covering my face.

"This wild hair of yours," my mother said. "Where did you get this hair?"

Some man gave it to me.

My mother's hair was always thinner, straighter. I don't know who I got my hair from, but I know it can't have been from her.

Some man.

More and more of the things we chose to do and the places we ended up going, the things we had and the things we used, were all because of 'some man'. What he'd said, what he'd offered. Some strange man and his open, giving hands.

I remember running down a hill in my Hello Kitty boots—the pink ones with those daisies drawn with black-rim lines. No, the boots were lilac. Or maybe that was the daisies. Kicking the dew off long blades of wild grass, my feet flying out in front of me in a thin spray of tiny water drops. Diamanté scatter. Hello Kitty flashing her mouthless, feline face at me from the top slopes of my encased feet, her expression benevolent under her slanted bow. My head throbbing as I slowed, so I pressed my hands to my scalp, feeling heat and grease and tight, tugging pain.

I don't remember which park this was. I only remember running down a hill towards the benches where my mother sat, watching. Sipping Coke out of a can through a thin, clear straw. Her shiny pink lips making pretty shapes.

"You feeling okay, babe? You look warm."

Calling me over to sit with her and Some Man. Her smiling friend, our long-lost uncle.

"Have some Coke."

Isn't she sweet?

What a gorgeous little thing.

Some Man smiling at me like he wanted to know me. Like maybe he already did. My hands bleeding sweat into Momma's shirt, his shirt, where I clutched at collars, sleeves. Sick from too much sugar, from the pain so thick in my skull, squirming on my mother's lap until she passed me over to sit in his. Stronger arms closed tight around me, a wider chest to rest my head. Fresh sweat salting the spice-scent of aftershave. Stubble scraping my forehead, my neck. Something about the combinations here—such specific smells and sensations— thickening my saliva so I couldn't quite swallow, making my heart beat too fast and my muscles clench in.

"You feeling okay, kid? You look a little done."

Handing me a small white pill that would take me out of myself so I could feel better, to let me fall asleep. The total, dreamless dark where all you do is forget. Bright days give way to secret nights. Waking after in different clothes, in a different place, with nothing in-between but a thin haze. My hair wet from a bath I don't remember taking, my day clothes swapped for soft, clean pajamas. Staring up at a ceiling I either knew, or didn't. On a bed or a couch I'd lain on before, or not. Or sighing awake on the backseat of a car, someone driving us someplace else, my head rolling heavy on my mother's legs. Where we'd just been and who we'd just seen all facts and faces exploding to dust behind us, vanishing to nothing as we moved further away.

It doesn't matter now. That's gone.

But it hurts so much. Why do I hurt?

A feeling between my thighs like I'd been sitting on hot pebbles. Half-circle bruises pressed into my chest.

There were always the parks. Right from the start.

On these weekend trips, these afternoon excursions, my mother kept herself simple, neat. She wore her dark sunglasses, her faded jeans. She wore tank tops and belts with nice buckles. She kept her hair up in a ponytail, looking fresh and pretty like the girl she still was. If some older women made any comments, she mentioned something about *babysitting*. Pulling me closer against her. When men spoke to her, she giggled and her throat flushed. She took small steps away from me. She put her hands in her pockets when people talked to her, to us. Hiding them away I always thought, to keep herself from fidgeting. Looking back, I guess she was really holding onto what she hid there. Keeping it safe, or keeping it ready.

"Momma, I want to go home."

"One day we'll have a home, baby. A home just for us. It'll be the most beautiful thing you've ever seen."

Taking my hand. Leading me.

22

"**D**O YOU WANT to meet one of our new friends?"

Carris, in those weeks before we left.

My mother was making waffles when she asked me this. She was standing barefoot in our big kitchen with its sticky wooden floors and its tricky taps, pouring batter into the iron griddle. The mix made a soft hissing sound as it hit the hot metal.

It was early afternoon—late in the day for waffles. Clem had left sometime before dawn without saying goodbye. Mom told me this last part the moment I walked in the room.

She didn't say goodbye to you.

"She's going away again?"

"Not *going away* again," Mom said. "Just *gone* away for the night."

Which night? How many nights? She didn't say if that counted the night coming or the night before. I didn't ask. If she was gone again tonight, I had stale popcorn and bad TV ahead of me, searching for my mother's smell in the cushions while she walked through darkness towards the gate. Towards . . . who? People she sometimes stayed with so long I'd be asleep again by the time she came back. I woke up happier this way, when she slid her arms underneath me and carried me to bed. Chuckling at my sleep-mumbles, smoothing a hand down the back of my head. Cigarette smoke in her hair and something sharp on her breath, the night creeping stiff alongside us.

Was this why Momma decided to make us waffles? To cheer me up? To make me not mind the lonely night ahead? I loved it when my mother and Auntie Clem made waffles. The floorboards and countertops would be messy-white with spilled flour and scattered sugar, the sink crammed with beakers and measuring cups and more bowls than could ever have been necessary. In the better days not so long before, there'd been a lot of laughter along with all the yelling. They both sounded so much more the same. We switched between them that quick. And yelling or laughing the waffles came up warm and golden in their square grid shapes, cooling hard where the syrup seeped. Insides soft and trailing steam when we cut them open with our mismatched knives.

The kitchen was neater this morning, and quieter. Nobody was laughing. No-one was yelling. There was no in-between.

"So since it's you and me again today, how about it? Think you'd want to meet one of my friends?" She said it brisk, said it loud.

I stared at her.

"One of your momma's new friends, babe. He wants to meet you."

"He?"

In my head I saw the guy who checked our car over every other week when we got fuel, his cap pulled low to hide the zigzag of shiny skin cutting back across his scalp. I saw the newsreader on late TV, smiling at me with his hair combed back and his papers held neat in his sure hands. The guy at the supermarket who made jokes with Clem. The high school kid at the ice cream shop who always blushed at my mom.

My mother was quiet a while, holding the waffle iron shut with trembling hands. I remember this so well. How her fingernails, painted red, had started to chip. That something about this made her hands look older, and somehow not-hers. "He's a lonely old man," she said. Something wrong in her voice. "He can be a friend for us both." Something hurt. "And I don't want us stuck out here, all alone and lonely all the time. We'll both go crazy. I don't care what Clem says."

All alone and lonely. It sounded pretty, the way she said it. Sad and small, but pretty. She'd said it before, and Clem had yelled her answer in a voice so loud and so sudden it scared everyone. My mother and me and even Clem herself.

You can't have it both ways, she said.

Like the things we want are all split paths. Like the difference is all in Left or Right.

My mother is a sleeping snake. A dozing dog. Step on her tail and she'll whip back round. All the worse on those nights when her wine glass was empty and her hair was heavy around her face. With or without drink, raising a voice to my mother doesn't shut her up. It smacks her awake.

Quit breathing down my neck! she yelled right back.

Such vicious imagery. Like when she was home, Auntie Clem was always at my momma's arm, too close against her shoulders, stealing her air. Hovering, smothering, denser than a shadow and almost as close.

Quit breathing down my neck.

The way those words went, I imagined I knew exactly how it felt. But I saw Clem, too—standing back a step, startled. Amazed. The anger in her face sliding over into hurt. Her hands frozen at half-grab, fingers splayed open in the air. A shadow losing its shape.

"Does he have any other kids to play with?" I said.

The kids I'd played with in the past. The hide-and-seek

girl in the supermarket, a moment of eye contact somehow starting an unspoken war; a back-and-forth series of ambushes set up and down the aisles. The boy at the counter ahead of us a few weeks later, the one who flashed his bag of M&Ms at me. Shaking his shiny-bright pack of smiling circles. Laughing at me with something ugly in his grin. And of course, I thought of the school bus kid who waved at me that morning down by the gate. A smiling face in a row of neon pink hairbands, bright-colored backpacks. The flash of light and color that passed me by as I kicked over rocks and looked for frogs.

"No kids, but he has some beautiful big dogs. One of them just had puppies. He said you can play with them if you want. If you're not scared of dogs." She paused. "Are you?"

The dogs I'd met before. The mutt I fed half a doughnut to while I waited outside the post office one calm afternoon out on the high street. Black and scrawny with a dry, pink tongue. The white terrier behind the black gate at the end of the road, barking insanity at any car that went by. I knew its voice so well I was surprised when I finally saw how small it was. How filthy and sad and somehow pitiful. And those two German Shepherds I saw in the back of a parked sedan one day, somewhere out in town. Collared but unleashed with the windows rolled wide open. Sitting rigid with their heads out in the air, black grins and curved fangs and happy, watchful eyes. Calm and powerful, like in their hearts they were more wolf than dog.

Was I scared of dogs? It was hard to know for sure.

"Anyway, I'm sure you'll like the puppies," she said. "And Steve. That's my friend's name. Uncle Steve."

"Is he nice?"

"Come on, babe," she said, sounding stung, though I couldn't see why. "I wouldn't introduce you to anyone I didn't think was *nice*."

Steam streamed from the edges of the closed waffle iron. *They're only done when there's no steam coming out.* She'd taught me that. Was this the kind of thing kids learned in school?

"Do you think he'll let me keep one of the puppies?" I said, sliding off my chair as I said this because I wanted so badly to jump up if she said 'Yes'.

It took me that long to forget the hurt in her voice. Which is, no time at all.

"I don't think that's a good idea," she sighed. Her voice was low and slow and even more wounded than before. "You see, I'm not sure how much longer we'll be living here. Maybe it's getting close for us to be on our own. You know, find our own home to live in. Make our own money, buy our own things. You and me."

I half-stood half-frozen, half out my seat.

"I worry about us," she said. "I worry about where we're going and what we're going to do. Meeting other people helps you find new things. New things lead to new things. Uncle Steve's been a good friend to me these past few weeks. He wants to help us. Maybe. If he can."

I didn't have my secret eye back then. It first burst out of me not long after—a crack through the center of my forehead, writhing there a while before it pushed out and opened wide. But now, when I remember this day—the first day *Uncle Steve* was mentioned—it burns like it wants to burst through my skull and swallow my brain whole. Eclipse my mind so I can't think or speak. A blast of vicious images, stuttering by before its gaze.

"It might be nice to have another friend," I said. My voice was small the way it always is when I'm not sure I'm saying what I'm supposed to. Like I want to gasp the words back down my throat, just in case.

The steam from the waffle iron was slowing down, thinning. The aroma in the kitchen was warm and sweet.

My mother turned away from me. I caught a glimpse of her lips pressing together. "Your best friend in this whole world, though, is still your momma. And will always be your *momma*. You know that, don't you babe?"

I nodded. Too fast, maybe. I sat back down in my seat.

She stood still for a moment then. Still and shivering, like a frozen branch trembling in a stiff wind. The smoke vanished, then reappeared. A moment later the scent of scorched sugar slid through the air.

23

I'M NOT SUPPOSED to smoke, you know. Mouthfuls of it, warm swirls hovering at the edge of my esophagus, burning like tiny fireballs on the way down. My lungs crackle open, seize. I choke back a cough, jets of smoke jolting out my nose in staggered silver puffs. I wait a moment. I try again. My hands already shake from the nicotine. The nausea comes next.

My mother has always smoked. Clem did, too.

"It's not a good habit for a kid," my mother has told me. "Staying away from cigarettes keeps us girls pretty." Winking. Sliding a menthol between her lips.

It started with the guys offering me cigarettes back when I was nine or maybe ten, eleven or maybe twelve. Handing them to me when my mother wasn't around, flicking open a box to show me a deck of slim, spicy-smelling tubes neatly packed in tight rows. The filters all clean as cotton without the scorch, the stain that marks them later.

Would you like one?

Something secret in their smiles.

Can you smoke?

Here, I'll teach you.

Take one. Here.

It's not just a rumor that they like the word 'secret'. That their second favorite word is 'special'.

You're special.
This is our secret.
Don't tell your mother.
Now shush.

Special things are silenced if people want them to stay secret. What's so special about something you can't tell? Cigarettes aren't so bad. Death row inmates always ask for them, as many as they can get. People offer them in bars, at rest stops. In places where they're in new company and they want to feel safe. It's like trading for love, only not really. Or maybe I just think too much.

I'm in the lot behind the supermarket. A wide square of concrete broken up in places, strangling the weeds in the cracks. A wire-mesh fence closing it off from the road, steps behind the building that stagger up in a metal grid. The brick wall behind me is solid, rough. I shuffle backwards until it catches at my shirt. I lean my head against it as the next flood of nicotine crashes through me in a spinning wave. My legs tremble on their hinges; hips and knees. With my eyes closed, it's hard to know I'm not tumbling through the space in front of me. Without the wall behind me, I wouldn't know which way is what. It would feel good if it weren't for the bolt of nausea swelling in my throat where the smoke just went down.

I exhale.

The rich, sick sensation clears after a few more moments. I open my eyes, and nothing around me has changed. Concrete, fence, weeds, wall. It's mostly quiet out here. My cigarette has burned itself down to halfway.

The fuckers put accelerants in these.

The memory of a man's voice blasts into my head, loud and clear and all at once.

The fuckers.

I don't remember who that was, or when. Something

manic in his voice: too much fury, too much bite. A homeless guy tweaking on meth. A drunk man raging at the walls. I think I've seen these things, before.

I drop my cigarette and crush it under my toe. The shakes and the nausea have hit me all the way into my guts and down my bones, and it's impossible to stand for now. I slide down to my haunches and cover my eyes with my hands. I don't know if I'm rocking, but it feels like I am.

When I drop my hands again, a group of boys are skating into the lot. They skid by me, road-scarred wheels ripping across the concrete. They look at me, but they don't say anything. Half-turns of their heads, eyes watching from the side. They wear loose t-shirts, long metal chains. Crucifixes, medallions.

I don't belong with them.

"Hey, girl."

He flips his board up under his arm and steps toward me. I want to stand, but I can't. The shakes hit me harder, but that's not the nicotine.

"Hey, girl. Are you okay over here?"

Sometimes I'm scared and I don't know why. Sometimes I'm scared when I don't have to be.

I raise my hand, nod to him. I smile. I don't want to have to speak. There's too much chaos jumping up and down my throat.

"You sure?"

I nod again. "Fine." The word slides out strong and loud like I'm not scared at all, like I really am *fine*. With this word, I almost feel it.

He stops far enough away, looking across at me. I stare back. He's fit, tall, slim shoulders and long legs. His skin is smooth and dark and clear, his wide eyes squinting jagged against the glare.

115

"We're just gonna skate here," he says. "Don't worry about us, okay?"

In his eyes, he sees something. Something that makes him careful, concerned. Even if I turn away, I'm not sure he won't stop looking at me, but it won't be in a bad way. He keeps his feet apart like he wants to stand guard. Protecting me, not his friends. Or maybe, protecting me from his friends.

"I'm okay. I'm really okay."

That's my voice this time: untainted and calm. I relax down into my feet.

He smiles and turns away, holding his hand out in a half-wave. His friends watch him, not me, as he walks back to them.

And it's okay. I'm okay.

I've met people like him before. The watchful, gentle kind. There was the old man on the train who sat across from me and didn't once call me over while he read me Roald Dahl stories, promising he wouldn't stop for as long as they made me laugh. The lady at the bus station who sat outside the restrooms with me while my mother threw up inside, shushing me through those tearing, retching sounds coming from the other side of the door. There was the man who took his envelope, then looked at the pictures and looked at me, and in that second there were tears in his eyes.

I'm sorry, he said. *I'm so sorry.*

It was a long time before I understood why.

It's not that there aren't good people in the world. It's that the bad ones are so much easier to find.

The lot seems brighter with the skaters around. Wheels growl and tear and rise to silence as the board slips up into the air—spins, smacks back to earth under wide-spaced feet.

There's laughter, and whooping.

They make it seem so easy—their fluid kicks, making a snake-like weave of forward motion. I think of vertigo, the fight for balance. That frozen moment when the board slips out from underneath. Smashed elbows, shattered knees.

"Don't let that happen to them," I whisper. *"Not to any one of them."* I don't know if it will work, but I feel better for saying it.

When I was younger, I thought up prayers like this all the time. Like whatever was in my heart would be strong enough to push away the bad.

I'm not thinking too much. I'm thinking things up. All the things I want to tell Susie. The things, somehow, I want him to know.

24

THOSE EARLY DAYS at the petting zoos and the public gardens, the nature spots and caravan parks. I remember them. Those hours we spent in the picnic areas where the shade fell over us in heavy, dark dapples. I kind of miss them. Those times we bought sparkly ice cream floats and bright red hot dogs and gave ourselves hiccups from laughing between swallows. Sitting out on the grass or at the wooden benches. Under the trees or beneath the sky. By the fire areas, at the camping spots. The scents of cut grass and scorched meat cutting over the dark, mud-smell of deeper soil. Momma's smile switching sizes, sometimes so wide I could see all the way to the back of her tongue, other times so small it was just a sloped curve. Her smile waxing and waning, her upper lip dipping in when her mouth stretched out. Lipstick marks on her teeth. Traces of red rubbed off on white. Smiling at something I said or did, something she noticed. Silly questions, a funny face.

It was summertime. Warm weeks spliced with days of rain. The wide sky and its clear, open blue calling people out from beyond their gated walls and routine paths. Everywhere we went, the parks were full of people. More chaos than quiet. Fat ladies in shorts with big cloth shoulder bags, their too-white skin singed to a bright pink by the stinging yellow sun.

Big men with sunglasses and bald spots standing around with their hands on their hips, their movements all in wide gestures—elbows out, fingers splayed. Shoulders rolling. Smiles pressed so deep across their mouths they might even have been real. They almost always had kids with them, the women and the men, together or alone. Small ones sitting on blankets with dumpy legs stuck straight out, puffy like dough rising in the sun. Little girls not much younger or older than me in breezy dresses that flew up when they ran, when they jumped. Bigger kids playing rougher games further out from all the picnic blankets and lawn chairs, the wide wooden bench-tables. Frisbees, balls. Squirt guns. Grass tearing under their feet, hair tangled into their eyes. Everything about them so loud and wild that the bigger people stood and shouted, stood and waved, shushing them. Cutting across those piercing screams, that roaring.

"You can't play with them, babe. You don't know them."

I still feel this same way now sometimes, when the music's really loud and I want so bad to stand up, to step into it. To dance in it. Want to, but instead sit stuck to my seat, my nerves flashing, the muscles in my thighs and shoulders twitching. Like there's a second me trapped inside my skin, one more alive with energy than I am.

Move.

Let me move.

Begging for this in the good way, not the bad.

It didn't matter if the kids I watched from my mother's side were laughing or crying—they always seemed happy. A kind of happiness that pushes through everything else. Even screams, even tears. On summer days outdoors, kids don't cry for long. Not even kids like me.

Move.

I want to move.

119

Muscles twitching, heart beating fast like I was moving, but I wasn't. Held tight against my mother's side.

"So what's your name today, doll?" she said. "I wanna be Taylor Elizabeth. People call me Tay or Liz."

Taylor. Or Liz.

"But your real name is prettier," I said.

"It's like a game, honey. Names aren't important. Not really. It's fun to change them sometimes. Makes you feel like someone different." She squeezed my hand, shaking me at the wrist. "So, who do you wanna be?"

"I don't know."

"There must be something?"

"I don't know."

Names aren't important. Not really.

So why was it so difficult to choose one? Say one aloud to my mother, say it like it's mine. Say it to a stranger like I've said it all my life.

Those strangers. The people my mother saved her biggest smile for. Her tight smile staining her teeth. That smile was for the lone men who stopped just short of us. The ones who watched us like they weren't really looking. Standing as if they'd forgotten how to stand—edgy on the tips of their feet. Their hands moving around their heads, messing up their hair. Dipping in and out of pockets, looking for something like they kept forgetting what. My mother's smile freezing each time her cheap plastic phone beeped. The one I wasn't allowed to play with. Siting up straight and pulling her hair back over her shoulder. Rising to her feet in a rush of warm perfume. Raising her hand to wave.

"Hey, it's your Uncle Dan!"

It's my friend Keegan.

Is that my Uncle Ben?

Calling them over to us.

"Hey, my name's Taylor."

Hi, I'm Cleo.

Magnolia.

Dolphin.

Blue.

"This is my daughter, Sadie."

My little girl, Petal.

This is Anastasia.

Lola.

Jean.

Because names aren't really important. Just a collection of sounds we give to each other. I guess any word or sentence is, really.

Nice to meet you, honey.

Hi, sweet girl.

Hello there, pretty thing.

A man in blue jeans and a button-down shirt. A gold chain resting in swirls of curly white hair. A guy with sunglasses on top of his head, dark blue jeans, dimples in his smile. Arms inked up from wrist to shoulder, covered in hair or shaved smooth. Breath like hot dogs, like beer, like peppermint. These men. Sometimes they blur together like they're all one unreal person; the type like most types that will vanish, dissolve into nothing the moment they turn a corner out of sight. Sometimes they meld, and sometimes they don't.

That man.

He sat beside me like a cripple easing into a hot bath—wincing on the way down, ready to flinch back up if it burned. He had long yellow teeth over too-white lips. They cracked pink when he smiled. He had a gold ring on his left thumb.

"You're the prettiest girls in this park," he said to us.

"Aren't we?" Momma said. Hugging me to her, my cheek pressed into the arc of her breast. Pulling her fingers through my hair in thick, gentle sweeps. Kissing the top of my head.

"Why are you shaking, Momma?"

"I'm just a little cold."

Shifting me up against her hips, lifting me up and away from her, towards the man who sat beside me. He smiled down and I smiled up—Momma's fingers tickling as they pressed into my armpits. I smiled back at him with mustard on the edges of my lips, ice-cream sticky-sweet on my chin. If I'd been wearing my mother's lip gloss, it was all gone.

And I said, "Hi."

Up close his smells clouded his skin, tainted into sweat. Soap and cigarettes, aftershave and talcum powder. Something sharp mixing with something it shouldn't. Razorblades scraping inside my nose, making me sneeze.

"Bless you, honey."

I didn't understand why he laughed—laughing like it's funny to hear someone sneeze. I didn't understand why he sounded nervous about it: my sneeze, his laugh, both. And not understanding, I laughed back.

Thinking, *The man. The man is scared.*

But seeing also he was excited—smiling. Nervous but happy all at once. His heartbeat trembling so hard against the place high between my shoulders so my skin broke moist with sweat.

My mother kept her hand tight on my thigh. She was smiling so wide and shaking so hard it was impossible for her to hide it. Her shoulders quaked round her shoulders, the shine in her hair flicked up and down as her head trembled on her neck. The smell of her adrenalin swirled up against her perfume and clouded the space between her and us. A smell like salt and floor bleach, blood and iodine.

I reached back toward her, thinking, *Momma. My momma's scared.*

Her hand tightened. Those fingers tensing like she was

ready to lean in and grab me back. To flinch me off him if it burned. Her touch not leaving me as other, bigger hands clasped across my stomach, closed over my knees. Wrapping me up tight.

"You're so little and light."

You don't weigh anything, nearly.

Is this a butterfly I'm holding here?

Laughing words, close, too loud against my ear. High and scared like it doesn't have to be. Stubble scraping the side of my neck.

"She's not so used to men's voices—"

"Oh, isn't she yet?"

That's a shame, that's a shame . . . .

That's okay, that's okay . . .

I like the way she wriggles.

I like the way she squirms.

Thick fingers twitching over my ribs, under my arms so I giggled. Big knees jerking up and down so I laughed.

"Hey, you like that?"

What a good girl you are . . .

. . . this is . . .

Lemme see your pretty smile.

And darker, too. Twisting in a moment: kiss to bite, touch to pinch.

I bet you're awful cute when you cry.

I knew for sure then what her hand was always there for. Why she never once stopped watching my face.

All these times, sometimes they meld together. Sometimes they can't. Beer and sweat and rough knuckles. Rough chins against my cheek, wide wrists locked between my knees. Birds singing over my head, kids laughing or screaming a few feet away. My mother's hands reaching for me, closing around me. Taking me back. "We'd better be going now."

One of our thick, square envelopes pulled from her coat pocket or out from the back of her jeans. Those square images filled with me.

"Give our friend here a present, angel."

Flash.

Even if I wasn't scared, she made me scared with that look in her face, that tremor in her core. Like a thousand thoughts were rushing at her and she was stuck holding tight. Another envelope handed back, from him to us. Laid down on the seat. A rectangle fold of paper dressed as a birthday card, a personal note, a pocket-sized gift.

Is a gift really a gift when they're swapped? When it's an exchange, is it really a present?

"Goodbye kiss?"

Is a kiss really a kiss when it's not about affection? When it's only about wanting to get close, to touch, is it really love?

Stubble-scrape and tainted saliva. Too hard, too tight, until my mother pulled me back.

"She's not used to being touched like that."

Let her go, now.

Give her back.

The place, the man, his lap. The chat, the push, the pull. Our envelope, his. The kiss.

A goodbye kiss.

"That's enough for a goodbye kiss."

Let her go now.

Give her back to me.

Please.

25

IF YOU WANT *life to be easy, you've gotta be a bit easy yourself.*

Advice from my mother when I was twelve, maybe thirteen. Old enough to need to know. Watching her snip the top buttons off blouses. Switch pale lipsticks out for red.

Even men who are intimidated by heels, like heels.

I've never worn heels, not even for a picture. My shoes have all been thin-strap sandals, Mary Janes, hiking boots. Beach slops, slippers. Once my mother made me two daisy chains, and wound them around my toes.

Everyone wants something beautiful.

She's beautiful, she knows. Taking care of her hair, careful getting dressed. Never looking another woman in the eyes. Like they don't exist, because even if they do there is still only *her*. There is only *us*. People don't call me *beautiful*, they call me *pretty*. With my plastic bead bracelets, my breath like strawberry chewing gum.

There are so many sad, lonely men in this world.

Always in her bag: mouthwash, a can of spray deodorant, a stash of ultra-thin condoms. Also always in her bag: two changes of underwear—one cotton, one lace—a Swiss Army knife, her old Polaroid and its packs of film.

The way you get a man to let you sleep in his bed, you make it clear he can do things to you in it.

My mother is the hero, the warrior, the angel. She learned all this the hard way so that I wouldn't have to. Not quite. Not in the same way. She says.

I was all alone, she says.
I had to do something, she says.
This is the world we live in.
And so it is.

***

My mother called herself Sally Oakley in the early days, for those first few months after we left Carris. *Sally Oakley* to sound like *Annie Oakley*, but not be so obvious.

"Sharp-shooting babes," Momma says. "No-one ever sees *them* coming."

That was the name she signed on the motel register, and when anyone asked she said my name was *Rainbow*. Because of course a young, dumb teen mom would call her child something like this. A pretty name, a joke name. A name better suited to a fluffy new kitten or a dapple-grey pony. You can almost see the big pink bow.

"God, you little terror," Momma tells me. "We'd only been on our own for a few weeks. You were still crying away every night for your Auntie Clem like she was your real mother, not me. I thought nothing would ever be okay again, the way that made me feel. You were breaking my heart so bad."

I don't know why, but it makes me happy. This idea of me hurting her. It means maybe I can do it again.

I was just a kid I was just a kid I was just a kid. Emotions on auto-tune, and always only focused in.

That night at the motel, Sally Oakley sat on the edge of the bed with its tumbled duvet and tossed pillows out of sight behind her. Tangled around her baby, her girl now maybe five or maybe six. Caught up in the mess, and crying.

"You were kicking my back. You were kicking my

126

goddamn kidneys. You were screaming so loud one of the neighbors started banging on the wall."

Young children do the nicest things in the nastiest ways. We're not supposed to regret anything. We're supposed to take the good with the bad.

Sally Oakley cried along with her daughter. If she'd been a little younger herself, she might have kicked her legs, too. She sobbed into her fists.

"You weren't hungry, you weren't tired, you didn't want anything from me. You were angry. So damn *angry*. Wanting your old bedroom back. Screaming for Auntie Clem. You wouldn't stop, I couldn't take it. I wanted to kill us both."

The word for this is *filicide*. It's a lot more common with single mothers on tight budgets. The younger the mother the more likely the act. I saw stories about this on someone's television once. The actors in the re-enactments looked too angry. I don't think it happens this way. I think it's more about tears and sobbing. Hopelessness clutching at their heads, getting into their hands. When talking about young mothers, it's not hard to see how it happens. All that youth and passion, bottled up in a dingy room and shaken to insanity by a screaming baby.

She jokes she wanted to kill us both, but she wouldn't say it at all if she hadn't thought about it. People talk a lot about how much mothers love their kids. I guess it comes in different forms.

The pocketknife in Sally's purse was an old Swiss Army issue, the kind with can openers and corkscrews and nail scissors attached. She still has it. We call it *Freddy*, like from the movies. The blades are notched so tight together if you try to pull one out and don't do it tough, it'll snap back and slice a finger before it locks straight. It's possible Sally thought about taking the knife out, that night in the motel. Thought about risking a little blood. And it's possible the thought got her contemplating carnage.

Or maybe that's unfair.

"There was a knock on the door. Not a banging, you know, not like the jerk who'd hammered on the wall earlier. It was polite, careful. Still, I was scared about who might be on the other side. When I didn't answer the first time, it came again. I figured, hey. What will be will be. And you were making so much noise . . . "

The woman knocking on Sally's door wore a uniform, slate grey, cut like a house dress. Her hair was pinned back and she wasn't wearing any makeup. She might've been forty or maybe fifty—more young than old, but with too many lines in her soft, tanned face.

I don't remember her, but I see her this way.

"That unspoken *Mother Code* thing was kicking in," my mother says.

I've seen this happen, so I guess it's sort of true. It's when a woman on a train takes a screaming baby from another. The way a lost child gets hugs and lollipops from the stranger helping look. How, when everyone else is glaring over at the kid throwing a tantrum, a few female eyes look back with sympathy.

I don't know too much about a *Mother Code*, but it sounds like a nice idea.

The Maid Lady, she couldn't finish her shift and go home like this. Not with the sound of a child's screams locked in her ears. Remembering the itching helplessness, the vicious fury a mother can feel—enough to shred the walls black and red, shatter and destroy. The opposite of giving life. The opposite of creation. Because having a kid is like dying in a car wreck. Because even though a woman doesn't die all the way when it happens, a part of her doesn't always come back.

See, I don't know this, but I know my mother, and I think I understand.

"She came in, and she was so great with you. She sat down by you and she pulled your head into her lap. You didn't stop crying, but you stopped the screaming part of it, and you stopped kicking."

Maybe I thought she was Auntie Clem, this woman not-my-mother coming into the room just to hold me.

I don't remember this night, but I know the feel of it.

"She told me to change my shirt and go for a walk. She told me she had nowhere to be that night, and since she'd raised three kids on her own she was pretty sure she could handle this while I got some space for myself. I could hardly think straight. She was like a patron saint appearing out of nowhere, only for me. So I did what she said."

Sally changed her shirt and fixed her makeup while Maid Lady looked for something decent on TV. An old-school movie or a cheerful, cheesy sitcom to help shush me down or drown me out, or something in-between. Sally put her lipstick on and zipped up her boots. She walked out, stung all the way to the nerves in her fingertips, every part of her singed and aching. She was still crying when she left.

"I remember how quiet it was, all of a sudden. Outside, away from the motel. There was a highway arch not far off, but the roads by the motel weren't so busy. The pavement was wide and the shops were well-spaced. I was alone enough without being totally alone. The wind was so fresh. I wanted to walk for hours."

The cars that went past didn't slow for her, didn't stop.

"It's a new feeling for a small-town girl, when you realize where you are now you're a total stranger. That you don't know anyone and nobody knows you. As scary as it is, it's also kinda . . . *stunning*. In the good ways as much as the bad."

The sign for a bar floated ahead, the letters bright and blurred because her eyes were still wet with tears.

"I'd never been out alone like this before."

My mother, she got no time between childhood and motherhood. No gap to be herself, as herself. Going for coffee with friends each morning like the perfect-looking girls on all those TV shows. Sipping espressos and talking about their cocktail nights and their office battles, and the handsome men with neat haircuts and dark suits who ask them out on dates. My mother would've looked good doing that. I guess as much as any mother loves her kids, she has to hate them a little, too.

"I have no idea what time it was, but the place was almost empty. There was one guy sitting by himself at the bar. I noticed him right off because of the way he was hunched over his drink—so sad and alone, like he could barely lift his head. He looked the way I felt. He was way older than me, but I didn't care. He was kind of forties-fit. You know the type. He had a faded t-shirt with LOVE THE DUCKIE printed on the front. See? That kind of thing makes it easy to remember. He let me cry on his shoulder and he bought me a beer. My makeup smeared all over his shirt. Then I spilled the beer down his front."

LOVE THE DUCKIE. His old high school band. These forties-fit guys, when they're the sad kind, they tend to be nostalgic about stuff from when they were younger men. Guys like him, they share a lot of the same. Some dream they never chased, some girl they never got. Or they're sad because they got the wrong girl too early, along with kids and credit card debt. When they visit bars alone, you know they're the type to be craving touch. That kicked-puppy smile behind their eyes. When they meet women like my mother, they're always glad to talk.

"He was so sweet about it all. He looked down at his shirt

and saw the black stains from my mascara. He could've been mad, but he looked kinda proud almost. I thought that was pretty cute."

Within five minutes of meeting my mother, she'd already broken his quiet evening out alone and stained his favorite old t-shirt. I wonder if he realized or if the intimacy of my mother's tears on his heart, the shock of cold beer in his lap, took him over like a bucket of ice tossed into hot water. Change the mood and change the state.

"You've got to understand, babe," my mother said. "There are a lot of sad, lonely people around. It means a lot to give them some light. Something special, only for them. Something they want, and didn't think they could get."

Mr. Duckie let us stay with him for a few weeks. It's not a place I remember. I guess I was still mooning about Clem, about wanting to go back to Carris.

Time to go.

Tension, irritation racking up each day. Goodwill burning off like water against a blowtorch, vanishing in a sharp steam. Think of a cat that's just vomited on the carpet. Picked up and tossed out the back door. Flung. *Unceremonious.* Mom and me have been thrown out of homes before. *Unceremoniously.* Stung skin and sudden cold, adrenaline blurring what we think and see so it feels like a dream.

Sweet Mr. LOVE THE DUCKIE was the first, but I still remember him for his goodwill as much as his loneliness, and the frustration that bit it down. Mr. Duckie was my mother's first *Friend.* The first man whose bed she slept in while I curled up in a spare bedroom, on an old futon, on an air mattress with patched-up holes. She says I slept between them sometimes—Mr. Duckie and her—on his black and blue bachelor sheets, in his low-slung queen-sized bed. But I'm not so sure. Maybe. Maybe not.

"In the time we stayed with him, I got us on our feet. If that hadn't happened—without me meeting him—maybe we'd still be standing street-side with our thumbs out. Maybe we'd still be stuck out in the cold in awful clothes. If that hadn't happened, my girl," she says. "We'd be a lot worse off than we are now."

Sometimes I'm scared when I really shouldn't be. Sometimes I doubt and I don't know why.

"The more money we make now," she tells me, "the sooner we can buy our own house, and we won't ever have to talk to anybody we don't want to. Ever again."

26

I DON'T KNOW where Susie is. Gone for the day with his *deliveries* and *grades*. Mom bolts the front door from the inside and drags a chair up against it.

"*Our* space now," she says.

She's hungover again, red-eyed. My mom, she can look pretty young even though she has to be around thirty at least, but when she's had too much to drink the night before, no amount of cleanser and hairspray can pull her youth back into focus. Her skin dries out and shows the crow's feet and fine lines creeping in under her eyes, shrinking the blue above. Her mouth curves down at the edges against her smile—her headache grimace, warping her mouth. Her color is too waxy, too grey. Concealer helps, but it can't change what's beneath.

We don't have a hairdryer, so I'm combing my hair and toweling it in turns. My hair slides wispy and damp between my fingers when I pull. The process is drying it fluffy, light. My skin is slick with lotion. I'm chewing gum, even though I don't have to. Strawberries in a toothpaste taint.

"You're lucky you got my hair," she says. "This color, and the weight. It's a shame we don't have a curling iron. You'd look so cute with baby-doll curls."

She's shaking out her makeup bag, tossing aside the reds,

the blacks, the things with thick tips and the things with too much glitter.

"I don't want to hide your freckles," she says. "They're too damn cute, but your tone needs some evening out." She's holding up the palest liquid concealer, considering it against my face. "Aren't you lucky you got my skin? I swear you've never had a zit in your life."

"Yes I have."

Just because it's a nice thing to say doesn't mean it's not bullshit.

"Oh, come on, grumpy," she says, widening her grimace-smile. "Let's have some fun with this."

It can be fun. It sometimes is. There was the time by that old dude's swimming pool, sunshine so bright it blurred out the flash. I was in and out the water, cool drops fresh on my darkening skin, squeezing chlorine out my hair. There was the time we mixed up Pina Coladas, sweet coconut and sharp alcohol loosening my arms and legs, helping me lie flat and easy, making me giggle while my head spun against the light.

Flash.

I don't like the wax strips. We had to start using them when I was around eleven, maybe twelve. I don't know, because I don't know what's normal. The ages these things happen to other girls.

"Let's try to freeze you at twelve today," my mother says. She's staring at my face, but not like she's looking at me. Not exactly. She's figuring out what we can get away with. "I love you, baby," my mother says. "And I want you to grow up into a gorgeous woman who puts on a pair of stilettos and *slays*. You will, I can tell already, but I wish it wasn't happening quite so fast."

There's worry in her voice, but that's not my fault. I look down at my body, still naked under my towel while the lotion sinks in. Cleavage, hips. Dips and arcs. I might be hairless, but that's where it stops.

"Your breasts are getting bigger, too," she says.

"I could care less."

"I *couldn't* care less."

"Whatever."

"*Grumpy* today," she says again, and I hear the strain in her voice. I know she's hurting, I know she's stressed. Too much booze the night before. All this puberty already passed. Right in front of her, right in front of us. We couldn't stop it even with our careful watching.

The underwear I'm going to wear today is new—white cotton with bright red cherries printed all over. There's a chance they're too small, but that's okay. Fabric in your ass crack, it doesn't need to look so bad.

The sensitive space between my legs is stinging from the wax strips. Tomorrow it'll all be raised in bumps and lumps and flares of red. I've rubbed Vaseline on for now. When we wipe it off for the camera, it'll sting.

"Okay. Lip gloss, concealer. That's it. What do you think?"

She's holding up a lip gloss labeled *Coral Pink*. The same shade as the soft, stinging flesh-folds between my legs. I remember the days when I loved putting lip gloss on, because the taste was sweet and I liked licking it off. Now it feels like grease on my mouth. I'd rather wear lipstick. I would.

My mother pretties up my face. It doesn't take long.

"You want some wine?" she says. "There's still some left."

"I'd rather have cocaine."

She laughs like I'm joking. "I'd let you smoke a little weed, if you want?" she says. "Susie gave us some, but it'll make your eyes red."

I don't like marijuana. It makes me think too much. It makes me see and remember things with thick emotional tones that burst through my brain and get my scalp burning. A strange kind of headache, throbbing at the thoughts inside.

I'm in an old pair of jeans with the legs cut off. The jeans don't fit me anymore, not really, and the zip won't close. Showing white cotton and bright red cherries.

"That's fine, doll. That works fine," my mother says.

I look at myself in the mirror before we go into the room, and my mother's right. I would look better with curls.

Susie's bedroom is big for the size of his apartment. It smells like old sex even with new sheets on the bed. The smell of my mother, and of him. Salt and sweat and something unpleasantly sweet, like milk just before it turns. The room is clean, though. At least there's that. For a guy, Susie's pretty neat. Clean nightstands, working lamps, a chair in the corner with a few old t-shirts thrown over the back. I've been in rooms with no sheets on the bed, stained mattresses glaring horrors no matter how we cast the light. Condoms, stray socks, junk food wrappers. Pushed into the corners or swept under the bed.

My mother pegs a white sheet over the window, something to smooth the sunshine coming through the other side. The room sears.

My body feels stiff and slick. I'm sweating underneath the layers. Grease from the moisturizer and clothes that don't fit. My hair dry as stripped straw, floating against my face.

"Come on, babe," my mother says. She's checking the camera. She's loading the film. "We can't waste this."

She's waiting for me to get onto the bed. She's ready, even if I'm not. It's warm in Susie's room, but my skin is tightening, prickling.

This is where he sleeps.

I don't know why, but I feel bad about that.

"Confidence, babe. Try to look . . . innocent."

I try to look innocent, I try to look confident.

I try to look confident about my innocence.

27

I WON'T LIE about what I do and don't remember. The eye in my forehead flutters like a black moth caught in a bad dream, fetching the images that shadow the back of my mind. Because the cliff-edge dividing what was and what is . . . the ink dot that bleeds in place before the line changes course. It starts falling down right about here.

We made waffles and we burned them.

And then my mother told me about Uncle Steve.

***

Momma was wearing her tan-and-sheepskin jacket, the one with the broken zip and the collar that flipped up against her ears. Faded and stained. It smelled the same way old books smell. She wasn't wearing any makeup except for her mouth— a darker shade than normal, the color like the inside of a wound. She looked young and pale and kind of still. Maybe it was the chill on her bare cheeks, the way her breath puffed in tight bursts of vapor. She was breathing like her jacket was too tight and she couldn't take air in all the way. She kept her arms crossed over my chest. Her knees trembled behind me.

I don't remember where I was when this memory first came back to me, but I see a ceiling bright with yellow-green plastic stars, shining down on me through the dark. The bed is narrow and soft. I'm not cold, but I'm shivering. It's the memory of cold that makes me shake like this. There's a pillow under my head and there are voices carrying from the next room. I'm here alone. I'm supposed to be sleeping.

"She could be your baby sister," Steve said.

We were standing by our car in a different driveway. The house was smaller than ours, with grey-white walls and weeds growing up around it. The windows were dusty against the sun's glare, and the front door had been weathered down to a slate grey with chips of faded red paint caught between the splinters. Everything old and wounded.

"We're only fifteen years apart, her and me," Momma said. The way she said it, it was like she knew he already knew it. Like she was saying it for something to say. To say something about me.

"Hey, little girl," he said. He held out a hand. His hands were enormous. The shape of them, stuck to the ends of his long, thin arms, reminded me of the garden shovels Auntie Clem sometimes used to scoop fallen caterpillars off the ground. Breathing through her nose as she dug under those slimy layers, her shoulder hunched into each scrape. "Don't be shy," he laughed at me. "I'm a friend of your momma's. I'm a friend of yours, too."

"Give Uncle Steve a hug," my mother said, stepping back with her hands behind my shoulders. The first time she held me out like that—tense, trembling. Ready to snatch me back up.

Uncle Steve's skin was loose with age, it rumpled over his neck in rolls that split to finer folds. Behind his ears, down his throat. He had almost no hair. His teeth were long and yellow with paper-slit gaps between them. His clothes all looked a size too big, and though I smelled soap and aftershave on him, I smelled something else there, too. Something low and moldy like chopped wood left for weeks in the rain.

She is damn crazy cute. You weren't kidding.

I don't remember what he really said, but my mind fills this in.

"Do you like iced tea?" He stooped down to say this, and when he spoke I smelled his breath. Cigarettes and thick saliva. Something medicinal and sweet, like cough syrup.

"We'd love some iced tea," Momma said.

"Come on, little girl," Uncle Steve said to me. "My bitch Leia had four pups the other week. Their eyes just opened. They're almost as cute as *you*."

He held his hand out to me, and I didn't want to take it. Not that big, heavy thing hanging off the end of his wrist with its hooked fingers, its swollen knuckles all sprouting hair.

Don't hate him cause he's ugly.

Clem told me a story once, about a baby duck that was really a swan.

'But what if he grew up uglier?' I had asked her at the end. *'What if he never got beautiful?'*

'We shouldn't be unkind to people because of how they look,' she had said. *'That's what the story means.'*

'But you're ugly and I'm not unkind to you.'

I didn't expect to see the hurt in her face. Kids are good at this: giving the nicest kind of compliment in the nastiest kind of way. Looking at Steve, I had a lot of nasty thoughts. But I was looking for the nice ones, too.

Don't hate him cause he's ugly. That's what Clem meant.

My nice thoughts made me feel sorry for him. His sad, small house, his baggy clothes. His old-man smell and his shovel-shaped hands.

A big, ugly swan, I told myself. *He's a big, ugly swan.*

I smiled up at him, and I let him close his fingers around mine. I let him lead us to the house.

"We still got a deal?" he said to my mother.

"Yes," she said.

"Don't back out now."

"I won't."

***

I won't.

I can't do it.

I don't feel like it.

I won't.

I don't remember what we were doing when I had this conversation with myself, but I feel a cool mist sliding across my face. My thighs are tight together, and I'm kneeling on the ground. There are hands cupping my face. Soft but strong, quivering like they might clench at any moment. Tighten on my jaw, press under my eyes. Break me, blind me. Another hand takes my hair back behind my head, a tug that might hurt but doesn't. I'm not afraid, but I know I should be. Instead there's a dull calm running through me. Like I'm the stillest of rivers, sliding low between the banks. Too steep down to reach.

The dogs were in a wooden box, shoved in the corner of the kitchen between the fridge and the back door. Leia was a large, brown, terrier type with stiff waves of wiry fur. She lay very still, spread out flat on a sour-smelling blue blanket. Her breaths were fast and shallow, her ribs pressing up against her skin in pulses. Her eyes were dull, glazed over. Her nose was dry. She flinched when I touched her, but that was all. She was scrawny as a dried-out prune with a heartbeat stuck in it, but her teats were fat and swollen. Plump beneath her thin skin, heavy against her bones. Like they were sapping all the strength out of her. I guess they were. The puppies were doing fine. Fat and round and warm and somehow boneless, the way their legs splayed out when I picked them up, limp and malleable. They whined in sing-song when I plucked them each off a raw, red nipple and held them up to my face in turn.

"That's Loki, the one you're holding," Steve said to me.

This puppy was darker than his brothers and sisters, with a bullet-shaped head and tiny, folded ears like soft pink sequins. I held him against my chest. He was firm and tough like foam rubber, moving in my hands. He smelled sweet and rich, like sugar boiling in milk.

"Usually mother dogs get angry when strangers pick their babies up," Uncle Steve said, standing over me. "They'll growl, maybe bite. Or they watch you with big eyes, scared you're gonna hurt one of them. Leia's not like that."

"Poor momma," my mother said, crouching beside me. "She looks beat."

I don't remember what was happening when this first came back to me, but I see sunlight shining through shut curtains. The curtains are bright maroon, or maybe they're dark pink and it's the brightness behind that changes the color. They don't quite meet at the top, and sunlight slices through the gap, sharp as a knife, bright and molten. I'm trying to duck away from it—the slice, the burn. Something is stopping me, like my shoulders are heavy, like I'm wrapped at the waist. The inside of my eyelids make a bright red, dizzy lights, a vortex spinning with white stars. Or maybe it's the light behind, changing what I see. There are warm tears in my eyes.

"Leia here got sick or something right after she gave birth," he said. "I don't know yet how bad it might've affected her milk. I've been trying to bulk her up, even trying to feed her minced meat and things—expensive things—but she's not much interested in food. I've been eating a lot of spaghetti." He laughed like this was funny, though I couldn't see the joke.

"Poor momma," my mother said again.

Uncle Steve took the pup back—plucked him away with a rough grab—and held him up in his thick, swollen hands.

"If he grows up to be the way I think he might, he's the one I'd want to train. He wouldn't be a bait dog. Not him."

I didn't like the look of Loki in this old man's grip, how weak and fragile he was in such big, rough hands. If Steve squeezed the pup too tight he would break those soft, curved ribs. Snap those malleable, bendy legs. Loki would scream and squirm and blood would run out of his nose. I saw this so clearly in my head there was a moment when I wanted to cry.

"Why don't you hold onto him a while?" he said. "If your momma says yes, I was thinking you might want to keep him."

"Hey kid, a *puppy.*" My mother, delighted. "What do you think?" My mother, laughing. A kid herself. She took Loki out of my hands, pressing his bullet head to her stained mouth. Smiling again. "I feel like I just had another baby," she said, and grinned at me, that grin for her and me. Steve missed it. Steve was the first to miss many things.

"You've got a good girl," Steve said to my mother. "Good girls get good things. Like puppies." He took Loki from her and laid him back down in my lap. Sweet, squirming thing. "Yours, little miss?"

I liked Steve a lot better, then.

I stroked Loki's silky head with a curved finger.

Mine. He'll be mine.

Steve got me iced tea. It wasn't in my usual mug—the one at home that was red bleached white, the ghost-words of *Happy Birthday* hovering in faded edges—but in a big, tall milkshake glass with patterns set in the sides like rows of hard bubbles. Ice clinked around inside. It came with a long, red and white striped straw, already curved over at the bendy part.

It's like from a movie. I don't know if I said this, but my mind fills it in.

Sometimes I'm happy and I'm not sure why. Sometimes I'm happy when I don't think I should be.

DOLL CRIMES

***

I don't recall where I was when I first let myself remember this. But the same lights are in my eyes, flashing shock-white so everything around them seems black. I'm shivering just as cold.

I won't.
I can't do it.
I don't feel like it.
I won't.

My mother bit her lower lip so hard she scraped all the lipstick off. My half-mouthed mother, taking me into a room with an iron-post bed with floral-pink covers trimmed with white lace. I remember it was like a girl's room, but wasn't, because the bedcovers were the only pretty thing in there. No desk, no dresser. No details, no signatures. A sheet of white plastic taped over the windows, making the light murky-bright. I couldn't see the garden outside.

"Try these things on, babe. These things we got for you."

A small green bathing suit in two pieces, long strings hanging off each part, tangled up into loops.

Puppet clothes.

I'm pretty sure I had this thought. Or I don't know. Maybe.

The room seemed smaller, the way they both smiled. So big and so wide.

"Don't worry about Uncle Steve, babe. He just wants a few pictures, that's all. It's a pretty swimsuit, huh? Maybe when the weather's warm again we'll go to the swimming pool like we did last year. You remember?"

I didn't remember. I didn't remember the pool. Only the smell of chlorine, and sharp pains in my ears. All of me shaking, my skin so wet.

But I'm cold.

"We'll get the room warm, okay?"

"Such a pretty little blonde thing," Steve said. "With that pretty little thing." He laughed. It was an ugly sound. Not like the kind of laugh I'd heard before. It bolted out of his throat like a blast of pebbles hitting an iron bucket. Too hard, too loud, scattering against the edges.

The eye in my forehead hadn't been born yet. Only the faintest opening stood there now, burning along its slit. If it had to widen, it would hurt.

Try these on for us, babe.

Flash.

It was a Polaroid camera. Steve gave it to my mother. I never saw Loki again.

28

W'RE AT THE pizza place around the corner from Susie's house. A takeaway spot with restaurant ambitions. Checkered tablecloths over plastic surfaces, fluorescent lights swapped out for candles melted into green bottles. The seating is too tight; tables and chairs crammed up against the counter where waiters do the ordering right over your head. The menu is written out in chalk on the blackboard up on the wall. Swirly letters all shaded skew.

Margherita, but not like the cocktail.

Regina, the name that makes boys smirk.

"And what's the little lady keen on?" Susie says to me. Smirking.

"She likes calzones," Mom says. "The more mushrooms the better."

My mother and I ate mushrooms together once a year or so back. The colors brightened up around us in booming tones, and the sand we lay on snaked in loops and patterns. I'd never understood before how everything is alive. Even dried-up water weeds. Even grains of sand. The moss growing vivid green on the rocks, it had a soul inside. It looked at me and smiled.

"I asked *her*," Susie says.

My mother's grin freezes. The way it stops on her teeth, I know it's not really a *happy face* anymore.

"I'm not hungry," I say.

Actually, I'm starving.

Actually, I'm ravenous inside.

My mother looks from me to Susie. Trying again to smile. "She's just being silly. Punishing herself or something."

"For what?"

My mother lifts her wineglass, a shrug twitching up her shoulder. "Teenagers. You know."

"Not really."

"Well, it's all pretty typical. Mood swings and stuff."

"Hey," I say. "Why are you talking like I'm not even here?"

Caught, my mother puts her glass back down, and I'm wondering how bad she really feels. I'm wondering why I'm getting *Mom Carded* in front of our new *Friend*.

"You got me, babe," my mother says. "Sorry. You have been a pain in the ass lately, though. I say that with all the love in the world."

The waiter comes out from behind the counter and walks the two steps to our table. His legs are too long for his body, and I see him slashed at the ankles as he steps. How that would be. An invisible knife, bolting out of the nothing and slitting his ankles, the backs of his knees. He buckles on broken tendons, flesh tearing open so fast it flashes white before it turns red. Blood slides out the slice marks, skin pulled back like open mouths.

I don't know why in this image, he suddenly isn't wearing pants.

I close all my eyes for a moment before I let myself look at anything again.

"You okay?" Susie asks me. He flinches at the elbow like he was about to reach forward. Try to touch my hand, my shoulder. Stopping himself too fast.

"Sure."

Susie orders me a peanut butter milkshake without even asking. "If you're not gonna eat, this is about as good as a meal," he tells me.

The waiter is staring down my shirt. I tilt my head back to make this easier for him. Almost all my eyes are shut almost all the way, but I like the feel of his on me. Something warm there, something frightening. My blood too hot in my throat.

It's not the waiter, not really. It's Susie watching the waiter. Watching the waiter watch me.

My mother has let her other *Friends* look at me before. Why should it be different with Susie?

By the time the waiter is done with us, my mother is blinking at me. Her forehead creasing up. Baby eyes trying not to tear.

"You look pretty in this light, Momma," I tell her.

She only likes candles because they make her look younger.

"I'm not gonna put up with this much longer, kid," my mother says. Because she knows what I'm really thinking.

"Hey," says Susie. "She's not doing anything wrong. Why are you acting like you're mad at her?"

There's a crack here. It's widening.

29

MAKE THE BLACK marker tumble down an inch or two. We kept moving. We stayed at roadside motels, the safer ones with clean-enough swimming pools and no used needles or wasted condoms lying around the outside steps. Not the ones that looked too rowdy for kids our age. The worse ones were always small and sour-smelling. Water stains on the ceilings. Mattresses sloped down in the middle from years of heavy bodies and not enough turning. The bathtubs were stained with yellow rings no human hand could erase, and the mirrors were flecked with small black spots like fleas frozen behind the glass. At night the sounds of people yelling, of TVs playing too loud. Sounds masking other sounds.

The check-out days, those were the best mornings. The quiet rush just before dawn. Momma ruffling my hair, dancing her fingertips to my armpits, kissing my cheeks to make me get up. Me giggling, kicking my feet, reaching my arms around her neck so she could pick me up and carry me to the washroom where a warm bath would be waiting, or the shower would be running, depending on what we had. After I was dressed she'd let me sit on the bed and comb my hair with my fingers, watching her pack up our things. She'd still be in a towel herself, knotted shut against her breasts. Her damp hair hung dark in messy twists, clinging to her shoulders, her back. I always thought she was most beautiful then: natural, in motion. Smiling at me in flashes when she asked me to throw her that bra, toss her that lighter—whatever was still cluttered on the nightstand or coiled up in the bedsheets with me.

Everything we owned, we carried around in our big blue duffel bag—jackets and shoes and bags, panties and shorts and skirts. Her makeup kit, some toiletries. Her Polaroid camera and its boxes of film. A few readers and coloring books for me: the more challenging ones, or the ones I hadn't finished yet. The ones I was done with we'd leave. I didn't have any toys anymore—those got left behind in Carris.

"You wear the heaviest so you can carry the lightest," she'd say, and put on her jeans and her knee-high boots, a clean t-shirt. She'd slide into her leather jacket if the weather was cold, tie it around her waist by the arms if it wasn't. She'd put on most of her jewelry too—at least, she'd wear most of her necklaces, and some of her rings. A few of the necklaces she'd let me wear, too. Plastic beads and leather pendants, things that spun and threw the light. She didn't let me wear the ones with glass or silver. Not the ones she thought I might break, the ones she'd cry over me losing.

We'd have it all worked out by the time we were ready to leave. The whole stay-but-don't-pay thing. Sometimes this meant sneaking out the back on a route she'd checked the night before, leaving the room key swinging in its lock behind us. Sometimes we didn't have to worry because an arrangement had been made, and we could walk right out the front. The guy at the desk still warm with my mother's kisses. Or his heart hammering against the Polaroids stuffed in his shirt pocket. Sweat bursting through his skin when it should really be blood. Acting, as he took it, like he didn't want to know what was inside. Except his eyes always said he did.

The thing with my mom back then—she was nineteen, maybe twenty but without makeup she looked more like sixteen, maybe seventeen.

Is that your baby, miss?

That can't be your baby.

There was the motel outside the desert. Flat heat and hissing sand.

The Setting Sun. That was the name.

The guy who ran it looked at my mother with such black fascination I could tell he scared her. The way she wouldn't look back at him, not directly at least. So unlike her to hide her eyes. The way she wouldn't stick around to chat with him, even when she was handing him money and he was trying to stare down her shirt.

We were eating pot noodles every night and watching television on a stuttering black and white. She kept a chair jammed up against the door.

I remember the nightmares I had back then. On those nights, in this place. The door shuddering, the chair bending apart. Me stiff on a warped mattress, too bare beneath stained sheets. Wet spreading into the firm, soft space beneath my hips, making the fabric stick to my skin. My eyes opening on a pure blackness, total and close. A blackness that breathed, that saw me. Scorching my eyes and filling my mouth, climbing into me through my ears, my nose, the fine pores of my skin. The door never opened, but he got inside anyway. The Motel Man. Hulking into the room with his long fingers spread, sharp tips probing the light he cancelled out.

Angel kid, he said.

I heard his voice, even if I didn't see him.

I'd wake up screaming, of course.

Momma started to think I was afraid of the dark. Shushing me in the neon-lit shadows, her arms damp and clammy where they closed around me as I screamed into her shoulder, thrashed against her, bit.

"I'm not dreaming," I screamed.

She says she couldn't make out my words.

"I know I'm not dreaming."

That's what I said.

"I'm not dreaming . . . "

The blackness clouding over, seeping deeper in.

30

WE'RE IN A suburb of a city somewhere, and the suburb's name is Rosefield. We're on the money side of the place, the part where everything is glossy and clean. Trash-free sidewalks lined with fancy cars, cafés with frilled awnings spread over outside tables. Trimmed trees and perfect flower bushes.

We got here kind of by accident, piling off the train after a lady who was hiding a kitten under her jacket. I caught the glimpse—bright green eyes mottled with brown, staring out at us from the shadow of a lapel. It tried once or twice to mew at us: tiny, bright-white fangs guarding a pretty, pink tongue. I say 'try', but maybe it did. The world can be loud for such a small voice, especially if nobody knows to be listening.

"Follow the kitty," my mother said when the woman stood, and jabbed me with her elbow. "*Hurry.* Animals are always a good sign."

I don't know about that, but maybe.

The cat didn't really matter, of course. Not if you're counting by 'signs'. Once we were on the street the woman was gone and the area looked good and my mother said, "Let's grab some coffee." Nodding to one of those bistro café things. Tiny round tables cluttering its section of the sidewalk. Lattes in fancy mugs. People in sunglasses and casual shirts with too many buttons undone.

The place is quiet, background music set to a low saxophone buzz. Or maybe it's Acid Jazz. I don't know.

I don't want to do this. Not in my denim jacket with the butterfly motif. Not with my candy-pink lip gloss. Not with my hair up like this. I could be twelve. Maybe fourteen. I don't have an office job. I've never ordered an espresso.

Even with a backpack over her shoulder, my mother stays sleek, looping it over the back of her chair like a laughing tourist at the end of a trip with too much money left to spend.

"Dry white wine," my mother says to the waitress.

She squints at her. "It's ten in the morning, ma'am."

"On a Friday."

She stares, hesitates. "It's . . . Wednesday."

"Can't you serve wine?"

"No," she fumbles. She actually blushes. "No, it's not that—"

"Great, a dry white wine and . . . " My mother snaps her fingers at me.

"A mocha, please. A big one. With marshmallows on top."

If I was wearing more makeup, if my hair was down, I'd ask for a Dom Pedro. Something sweet like dessert that would make me dizzy at the end of it. I don't try this here, today. Not in my butterfly jacket, not with my plastic-bead bracelet.

The waitress smiles at me like she's sorry for me. Maybe I'm not much younger than her. Maybe we're the same age.

I don't know.

She leaves.

"Hey, what's with *you*, sourpuss?" my mother says, mocking my expression back at me. Cartoon frown.

"I'm just tired."

"You've been off for *days*. You mad at me about something?"

"No . . ."

"Well, Sulky-Sue," she says, throwing her chin into her hand. "Remember life is supposed to be about fun. I'll sneak you some wine. You want?"

Yes, I want.

"Sure."

When we get back this evening, maybe Susie will be home.

"Men who wear loafers are begging to be castrated," my mother says, tilting her head to a guy a few tiny tables over from us. Widow's peak and loads of gel. Reading TIME magazine through his blue-tinted shades. The small, shiny type that are probably prescription.

"They wouldn't be so bad if they had laces," I say.

"No, babe. Castration. Either way."

I sometimes wonder if she actually hears the things she says. I'm literally half her age and I know better.

"Sourpuss," she winks at me. "C'mon, it's about time you smiled."

When our drinks come, my marshmallows have been melted and whipped to such high peaks it's impossible to take a sip without painting my face. My mother is checking her phone, and the thought of the Blue Shades man's scrotum getting hacked off and stored in his loafers has already crossed my mind a few times. All that blood flooding down his crisp, clean pants. Screaming as he grabs between his legs. The eye in my forehead is fluttering under my skin, too dark and too willing to open itself wide. Ready to show me. Always trying to show me these things.

I don't wanna see it.

Stop showing me.

Stop.

DOLL CRIMES

***

My mother sits back on the wide leather couch, and it's softer than it looks because she sinks right in as it molds around her. I take one of the armchairs alongside. The man who lives here, he's got good money, and there's no way he has a girlfriend. Everything lean and clean and shiny, hard surfaces and minimal trim. No scent of a woman, no trace of anything like a girl. His nightstand drawers would make for interesting exploring. Lubricants, magazines, toys. Polaroids. More.

But maybe we're not here for that.

There's always a still, cold curiosity when coming into a stranger's home the first time. It's like stepping into a museum, a place crammed with details and relics and tiny, coded infographics. There's a moment on entry when each new guest slides into open-eyed silence. Hands in pockets, or hands behind back. Taking in the rugs, the paintings. The toaster, the television. The words LOOK BUT DON'T TOUCH hover, invisible, over each wall and above every door. Each corner and surface is an open exhibit. The ashtray crammed with half-smoked cigarettes. The coffee mug waiting next to the sink. The empty pizza boxes piled up by the door. Color schemes, artworks, or the lack of them. The appliances the host does and doesn't have, what's broken and what's not. These things give a lot away. It can get overwhelming, just looking. Like I don't know if I'm nervous, and don't know if I should be. The only way to find out would be to break something.

Sometimes I prefer the places that are a little less perfect. Messy living areas and unmade beds. Half-torn posters and mismatched coffee mugs. The bathroom gives away the most. Although that Cleanliness and Godliness thing, they don't always have so much to do with each other. Tide marks, toothpaste-splattered taps. Bone-dry soap bars and footprint-stained shower mats. Someone who doesn't notice the details of himself. Clean hand towels, gleaming toilet bowls. Someone who's got things under control. If there's potpourri around somewhere you know a woman lives there, or did not too long ago. If there are a million shampoo bottles lined up on the shower floor, gummy and battered and squished flat, she's probably still around sometimes.

There was the man who lived above his hardware store. No curtains on the windows, and a door that opened up to the rooftop where he grew his herbs. It was cool out there, and calm. There was the guy who lived in a cottage behind his mother's house—hotplate life, his TV-stand crammed up against the foot of his bed so the picture flickered across to us, images and voices too loud and too close. The man with turtles in his bathtub; tiny, helpless things with curved flippers flapping over each other in the shallow, rust-colored water. He never told us what he was going to do with them. I've thought about it sometimes.

Our host for today's place is big, stripped down. Solid-color rugs laid down on clean tile. Charcoal grey and oxblood—woven, not fluffy. There's a flat-screen TV mounted to the wall. A couple of crafty-looking ornaments; sculptures of people, I guess, except they're rounded off in all the wrong places, stretched out in others. Bulbous heads and liquid-looking surfaces. I wonder what he would do if I picked one up and threw it at one of his walls. I wonder how much that would cost.

"Drink?" Car Dude calls from the kitchen.

He's a lot like Blue Shades, so much so that a part of me keeps confusing them. He paid our bill—three glasses of dry white wine, my mocha and a cheese board—and picked us up in a vintage Dodge Challenger. He isn't wearing loafers. Still, the image stays.

"Whatever's long and hard," my mother says, and giggles.

She looks at me with her happy, cheeky look that says don't worry—she'll share.

There's a second of silence, then startled laughter from the kitchen.

"Nice pad, huh?" Mom says under her breath.

It's okay, I guess.

I lift my feet up, but she stops me.

"Shoes!"

I pull off my boots and cross my legs underneath me. I watch my mother fidget with her skirt, plucking at the hem and then sliding her hands to her knees.

"Can I get your . . . *friend*? Anything?"

"My daughter. She's fine—she can have some of ours."

Car Dude comes back towards us, a tall cocktail glass with something orange and sparkly in one hand, a tumbler with scotch or whiskey in the other.

"Underage drinking," he says, smiling at me out the side of his eyes.

"She's supervised. C'mon. Kids are gonna do it anyway."

"You've got a cool mom here," he says.

"The best."

My mother hands me her glass first. I start with a small sip, but it's fresh and sweet and I like it, so I take a few bigger swallows before I hand it back.

Car Dude is awkward now, standing over us with a hand in his pocket, the other so tight on his drink I'm waiting for the glass to shatter. Sharp shards, ice. Booze and blood. All over his clean floor. Another layer of shine on his tiles.

"So what now, ladies?" he says. He's talking to my mother but he's still watching me. Those glances to and back that tell me where his eyes want to stay.

"You got any Oxy?" I say.

He laughs. "Oxy?" Then stops. "Wait, really?"

"Life is pretty breezy on Oxy," I tell him. I say this because it's something I heard once somewhere before. It made sense at the time.

"I don't mind her taking it once in a while."

"You're in luck, kid," he says. It's the second time in a row he's called me that, which would be okay if there wasn't so much insecurity around it. Or maybe I just think too much. "I've got the syrup, though, not the pills. Good news is the syrup works faster." He winks at me like I'm five.

My mother leans between her knees to unzip our backpack. She won't look at me again until I'm a little high. So I know what the two of them have said. This entire conversation, it probably started weeks ago without me. Car Dude isn't a friend of hers. He's a friend of a friend of a *Friend*. The cat had nothing to do with it.

I don't need Oxy, but I do want it.

He's going to want me to take my clothes off. He's going to lay me out on his bed. I know by the way he looks at me that this is what he wants. I know by the way my mother won't look at me that this is what she's agreed to.

It doesn't have to be so bad. It doesn't have to be so hard.

I close all my eyes.

You can't hate someone for hurting you. Because then you'd have to hate you for hurting you. And then you wouldn't have a *Friend*, or a friend, in the world.

158

31

I DON'T KNOW why I remember this night so clearly. That night we walked for hours, back when I was nine, maybe ten. Leaving someplace we would soon forget, heading toward someplace we'd never remember. The open world vacuous around us. It was dark, and we were cold. My mother stepped slowly for me. Shadows close around her feet, blooming then vanishing like blood spills seeping in and out the concrete. I looked up at her bare throat, the underside of her chin. The tips of her eyelashes clear against the curves of her cheeks. Her hair, recently dyed red, flared a cherry color as we passed beneath the streetlights. Momma walked street-side, and when the cars rushed by some of them blared their horns and flashed their lights.

I would've been afraid, except I was with her.

I should've been afraid, except I wasn't.

"It's not always going to be like this," she said, and paused to let a car rush by before she spoke again. "One day you and me will have a nice house and a pile of money and anything we could possibly want."

"What do we want?"

She smiled and glanced down at me. "No, baby. What do *you* want?"

Even now, when she asks questions like this, they're a kind of challenge. I had to think for a minute.

"A bright blue backpack," I said. "To put all my things in."

"We'll have a *house* to put our things in," she said. "Think bigger."

When I looked up away from her, the streetlights hit my eyes. Each one a sharp yellow glow with tiny black insects buzzing against its brightness. Small dark hailstorm. Beyond the lights, night swarmed the rest of space.

"I want a bedside lamp that looks like an angel. It'll sing to me when I sleep so I only get good dreams. I want a big bed, one with poles on each corner."

"A four-poster," Momma said. "That's called a four-poster bed."

"One of those. And I want hot chocolate and cake for breakfast, and lots of purple dresses."

"Purple?" Momma laughed like she was surprised. "I thought your favorite color was blue."

What my mother didn't remember. The little girl on a train with us a few weeks before, she was dressed in a shiny purple dress and she had a plastic crown on her head. It was painted silver, but the paint was peeling off. Cheap glitter shine. She sat by the window watching the hills change while her momma read a book. The girl was smiling, playing with the edges of her shiny purple skirt, sliding the hem up and down her thighs. The fabric made a shushing, crackling sound as it moved, almost as pretty as the color itself.

"Don't lift your dress," her momma said, and put a hand on her daughter's arm to stop her. Purple Princess looked up at her mother, the edge of her skirt still halfway above her knees. And she smiled. She was wearing lipstick too—a cranberry stain mostly faded, smeared around the edges of her mouth. She was wearing her mother's lipstick, just like me.

I still liked blue, but maybe more for backpacks. I wanted a dress that shone that shade, made that sound. I wanted a silver crown and cranberry lipstick. I wasn't sure how much of this was okay for me to tell my mother. I understood already we didn't have much money for those kinds of things.

"I *do* like blue," I told her. "But I like purple, too. Especially if it's a dress."

A car came over the rise and roared towards us, flashing its lights in blinding bursts. It screamed as it tore by, and Momma's hair swirled around her head in a scarlet halo.

"*Fuck* you," she yelled at the car—words I almost missed over the roar, the scream.

"Why fuck him?"

"Because he could've stopped." She was holding my hand too tight, choking my fingers. "He could've stopped, instead of being a jackass about it. But it's okay. One of them will." Her voice was as tense as her grip on my hand, and for the first time in our walk I felt my stomach lift, uneasy. I realized maybe this wasn't just another evening stroll. Maybe we were in trouble, and Momma didn't want to tell me.

We followed the street around a corner, and the road we turned into wasn't as wide or as busy as the one we were leaving behind. Her hand relaxed and my fingers warmed with a rush of new blood.

We walked for a long time before any more cars passed us. The streetlights seemed dimmer, or maybe the street was darker. It was late and my feet hurt and my legs were tired. I wanted to stop walking, but Momma's steps stayed steady. *Pock-pock.* Heels on the concrete. Hard steps. Blood spills.

"Sometimes," she said to me, "you have to be strong through the bad stuff because it means good stuff is just a moment away. Sometimes if you don't get through the bad stuff, then you don't get to the good stuff either."

"I know, Momma."

The lights gathered over a building up ahead. There was a

big digital sign with numbers all over it. We got closer and the buildings peeled away and there was a shop set behind a small parking lot with pumps and oil marks, and fireflies dancing through the overhead lights like stars warring darkness.

"Fuel," Momma says. "People have to stop here, even if they won't stop for a woman and a little girl walking alone late at night." Something so bitter in her voice, like she couldn't swallow.

She let go of my hand to dig through her coat pockets. The clink of loose change. "We can make a plan with this," she said. Then she smiled, dropped her arm around my shoulders and hugged me close to her as we walked. "You and me, we can make a plan with anything."

A purple sedan stood under the lights and the swarming fireflies. A man with a cap was filling his car. Something too-thin about him, like the monsters in his eyes got some of the flesh off his bones. I didn't see his face up close, but this is how I remember it.

A purple sedan.

A man with a hat.

A purple car, not a purple dress.

A cap, not a crown.

A man. No girl.

"Hey," Momma said. She raised her hand.

"You girls need some help?"

Later I sat in the passenger seat while he and my momma talked in the back.

"Close your eyes, kid."

I think he said that to me.

"I wanna taste your pussy."

He said this to my mother, in a low-moan tone rich with excitement. I didn't know what that word meant to him. *Pussy.* He slid the word *Taste* so tight between his teeth.

"Don't look, baby," my mother said, shrugging her jacket off and reaching forward to throw it over me. "Don't look."

I don't know why I remember this night so clearly. Sliding off the seat and onto the floor, small enough to fit. Making myself as small as possible, with my momma's jacket pulled over my head. My mother making sounds behind me like she couldn't breathe right, and was trying not to cry.

Push through the bad stuff to get to the good.

She said.

It won't always be like this.

She said that, too.

32

PHOTO ALBUMS. Do people still keep those? I've seen them more in movies than in real life. The movies have it wrong, too. Movie people have much nicer albums—they're full, they're glossy, like the pages get turned a lot. The albums I've looked through in strangers' homes are sparse. Heavy, hardcover slabs of wasted pages. They hold a few old baby pictures, shots of grandparents, of long-ago weddings. Maybe a couple of unremarkable houses, a double-page spread of holiday shots. The albums are usually stored at the bottom of some bookcase or stashed in the back of a cupboard. Shoe-box corners. They're always covered in dust.

We don't have an album, but we do have pictures. We keep our special ones snapped up with rubber bands, hidden down the side of our blue bag. The big one we stash at post offices and supermarket coat-checks, or lock up in hotel rooms, slid under the bed. It keeps our pictures safe among our collection of shoes and jackets and coats, the stuff we take with us, the things we keep. These pictures are Polaroids too, of course, but not the other kind. The oldest are from right after we left Carris—after we jumped across the country, motel to motel in a steady glide, living off the money from Uncle Steve.

My mom wasn't so great at managing money back then.

164

The first few places we stayed weren't like the places that came after. The first picture was taken in our room at that guesthouse where breakfast was free. Bowls of yoghurt, sliced fruit, eggs whichever way we wanted them. There's a picture of me standing by our window there, pink frill-curtain frame. I'm wearing Care Bear pajamas and my hair is straight and loose. I'm making a face, my lips pressed tight together and my eyes squinting. I'm hiding a gap-tooth. There's lip gloss smeared on my cheek.

In another picture, I'm riding a pony at a local market, smiling high. In the next, I'm cuddling a baby lynx at a wildlife sanctuary. Those are the best two. Most of the rest are shots of me in parks. Sitting under a tree, lying back on the grass. Eating a hot dog, my face dirty, my hair tied back. Posing on a rusty carousel with the sun in my eyes.

The pictures of my mother and me together are all at arm's length, a blind angle that cuts the side off a face, trims a chin, caps the eyebrows. With our faces so close together, it's easy to see how we look the same. Even the shape of our lips. The edges of our teeth.

My mom likes taking pictures of bridges. We've kept the really nice ones—a black arch with the sun behind, bright beams of light splayed to the edges like a giant starfish. A highway pass-over, calm and fresh at dawn. Smooth, cold concrete shining dark with dew.

There's a picture of her at an outside restaurant, a glass of white wine sparkling in front of her. There's a picture of her on a motorbike, posed like she can ride. Maybe she can, I don't know.

There is one mystery picture in the whole bunch. It's taken from the ground, angled up to capture my mother and me sitting together at the top of the highest kids' slide anyone ever saw. I'm sitting in her lap. Our legs are out straight in front of us, and her arms are wrapped tight around my waist. There was an age restriction on that slide, or maybe it was a height thing. Either way, I was too young or too short to go alone. I'm safe up there with my mother, and she's laughing into the clear air. I'm very young, but it's still me. My mouth is open in a kind of scream, but it doesn't look like fear. My eyes are too bright.

If the camera could dip down, it would show the other slides in the background. There were dozens of them, all different heights and sizes. Some of them were low, the top framed with the colorful cartoon-mold of an animal head— an elephant or a lion or a whale. Something smooth and open-mouthed. Some of the other slides looped and turned, a gravity pull shaped in serpentine. Climbing the ladder to get to the top would be too much for some kids. So much strain on thin wrists and shaky legs, fighting vertigo and bad coordination.

I remember this park well because we went there a lot. We went on weekday afternoons, late, later than the local kids, I guess, because by the time I was free to run and play, there weren't many other people around and the sun would be low in the sky like night was coming soon. Because it was. There were benches and picnic tables set out in the middle, each slide standing in the background like a monument, like a dare. The slide we're on in this picture was the tallest one. It was painted red—a color that screamed against the shade, against the shadow. Screamed like a fire engine, like a stop sign rushing up too fast. You knew just by looking how it would feel racing down from such a height. Everything whipping by in a few seconds that stretch forever—heartbeat stuttering, stomach bouncing like a rubber ball.

The slide park was the first park we spent time in, back when my mother and I were new to being alone like this,

166

unanchored. When I thought *any day now* we would go back to Carris. *Any day now.* I was still saving things for Clem. Motel stationery, wild bird feathers, drawings I did on the backs of receipts. I took a pinecone from under one of those slides. I wanted to paint it blue.

"You're not scared, are you?"

You're not scared.

Me and my momma climbing the ladder to the top of the slide, me caged by her body. Step, up, step, up. Her feet moving behind mine, nudging me from rung to rung. Her fingers whitening on the next bar above, her breath huffing into my hair. Her belly, her breasts, curved against my back. The ladder took us onto a square platform, and from there it was like the sky had gotten ten times bigger and the ground a hundred times smaller. I stared at the tops of the pine trees, shaking like I felt the way the world spins. I'd never seen treetops from the side before. The upper branches feathered out in fragile tusks, trembling in the breeze. If the wind blew strong, they would turn into tethered whips, lashing around against each other. Bleeding sap and shedding needles.

"Beautiful, huh?" she said.

Beautiful.

The mouth of the slide was wide and curved high for her to rest her arms up on its edges with her legs straight out. So all she'd have to do was push, and she'd speed back down to the ground. Leaving me alone at the top of the world with the wind and branches around me, weathered wood bending beneath my feet.

"C'mon, I'm not leaving you."

She braced me in her lap.

You're not scared.

My throat swallowed my scream at the sudden *whoosh* of air in my ears. We streaked down, gravity yanking us faster.

Momma's scream sharp and short and loud against my ear, cresting into a giggle. We were both laughing when we reached the bottom, sliding out to a slow stop. Our hair thrown around our shoulders, our cheeks red, our hearts humming. Holding onto each other, not ready to stand.

"Wanna do that again?"

That was fun, Momma!

I wanna go again.

Mostly I think I just tried to breathe.

The picture of us at the top of the slide, it's the only one we still have from that park. All the hundreds of others we took there—I think they got lost along the way.

Pictures are for happy memories.

You look so pretty.

That's my girl's beautiful smile . . .

Flash.

Me in dungarees with my arms stretched wide. Me hugging a pine tree, my hair pulled to the side so it loops over my shoulder in a golden spray.

Flash.

"What a great picture. Come see how beautiful you look."

My mother's wrist flicking, shaking the picture to make the colors rise. The ghost image of me, sharpening clear.

I'd like to find the slide park again. I want to go back because I'd like to remember. If we went there alone, and we made no friends, then who took this picture? This person my mother was smiling down on, this person I was laughing over at. The stranger who captured the moment before we launched.

If I don't remember who took this picture, then what else did I forget?

Flash.

I'd like to go back to that park someday. If it's still there, of course. I mean, it could be a parking lot now.

33

I WAKE UP to the sounds of mom and Susie fucking. Specifically, I wake to the sounds of Susie fucking. The sounds my mother makes are nothing compared. I lie still for a moment, stiff and uncomfortable on this filthy couch, in my too-tight jeans, my eyes swollen from sleep and my hair tangled around my throat. I'm nauseous and slow and scared to move. There's revolt in my body, it's rallying forces. Like the second I stand, I'm going to throw up. Like the moment I think clear, reality will kick me in the gut.

I nestle down and doze again for a while. When I open my eyes a second time, Susie is walking past me in his boxer shorts. No shirt. His gut is taut and firm, tough fat over tougher muscle, softening his lines. Not the other kind of gut, the heavier slap-barrel type that traps you down at the hips and thighs and makes you feel like you're caught in a compressor. Crushing you, pounding through and around in smothering shudders.

Susie wouldn't be like that. It wouldn't feel like that.

He's trying to slip past me when I sit up and say, "Hey."

He meets my eyes and his widen. Bloodshot, but sharp.

Over on the kitchen counter, his cellphone starts ringing. He nods at me, then vanishes to answer it. He smiles before he goes. A glance over his shoulder. When he smiles, I see his dimples—small depressions gathering his stubble into dark dots. One in the middle of each cheek.

"Good morning to you too," I say to myself instead of him, and smirk into his foul-smelling pillow.

When a man smiles at me this way. Even if it's over his shoulder, even if it's half-masked. When a man smiles at me this way. I know what that means.

***

There are a lot of things *Susie* and the other *Susie's* we meet don't see. Even when they tell me I'm *wonderful. Special.* How *beautiful* I am to them. These things people say before they think what they mean.

Susie's still on the phone when I walk into the kitchen. I go barefoot and bare-legged, t-shirt, jeans peeled off, leaving the seam marks pressed into my skin. He looks at me and turns his shoulder, cupping his free hand over his phone like it makes any difference. He's irritated, but that's okay.

I wait for this person who's calling him to stop asking him questions. All this stuff about *Deliveries* and *Grades.* Susie watches me as he talks, watches me like he's worried, uncomfortable. Something unsure.

It's okay, I've never understood much to do with numbers.

"Hey there, pretty girl," he says when the call ends. "You making coffee or am I?"

"You do it," I say. "I don't know where everything is."

"Lame excuse, my doll." He opens a cupboard. "Mugs." He opens another. "Coffee. Sugar." He points to the appliances by the stove. "Kettle."

"You probably make it better."

"Straight to the ego-stroke. Nice move." He grins like he means it, and hits the switch to boil us water. "So, when's your mom taking you back home, to school?"

"Mom says I don't need school."

"Well, even if she's right, she's wrong. Life's a lot harder without an education. Your mother should know that. Huh?"

He's saying what he thinks he's supposed to say. There's nothing in his voice like concern. Only easy curiosity, early morning conversation between strangers. There's something about sharing a roof that makes the people under it think they need to chat like they're friends, no matter how short a time they've known each other. He's talking like he's comfortable, but he won't look me in the eyes. It's my t-shirt maybe. It wraps me in a cloud.

"Did you know, once when my mother was high on ketamine, she told me I didn't have a father?" I say.

He stares.

"She told me I was a pure child of God, that what happened to her was a holy insemination by a figure with a face she never saw. She said this being gave her the most intense orgasm she ever had in her life. She says she came so hard, she knew she had to be pregnant. Just like that. She knew."

"Jesus," Susie says. Behind him, the kettle grinds toward a roar. The sound is like hailstones hitting hard soil. A sound I remember from Carris, I think. The hailstorms, not the kettle. The memory, not the sound.

"I've never had an orgasm before. Or, I'm not sure. If I had, would I know?" I lean on the counter by the door, hard on my elbows, pulling my hair straight with my fingers. I don't know if he's looking at me, but I think he is.

"I think that stuff isn't always as easy for girls," he says. "You're still a virgin anyway, though, right? I mean, you're not . . . not . . . "

I stare back at him. Because I don't know if I am.

"Jesus," Susie says again.

"Once we were on a bus and this man kept staring at me.

I was five or six I think. Young enough not to really understand. I asked her if I should go sit on his lap. I guess I said it too loud. That was the first time I saw my mom scared and angry with me. Like, both at the same time. She made us move cars, and then she made us get off at the next stop. I didn't understand why she was scared, or angry. Or both. Do you?"

He doesn't need to answer.

"She told me, 'sometimes what affects you infects you'. She told me, just because her friends like me to sit on their laps didn't mean I had to do it with everyone. She told me, not everyone. Not total strangers, out in public."

"Is that so," he says. His voice is flat. Like what I've said means nothing.

"Yeah, that's so."

The kettle growls down to a boil and we listen for the final seconds before it clicks off. It's the loudest thing I've ever heard—*hiss, click*. The end, the beginning. I watch Susie make us coffee. His hands are steady, but he still won't look at me.

Look at me.

"Your momma, she told me she's really worried about you," Susie says.

"Is that so." The way I say this, it's not a question.

"That's so."

"How drunk was she? How high?"

He sighs. "I have a hard time believing you, kid. Your mother, she's crazy. I can tell. Maybe she's done a few things she shouldn't do. Not with you around, I mean. But she loves you. She's just trying to keep you safe. I get it, why she says she's worried about you. If you're saying bad stuff like this about her, about someone who loves you and wants to protect you. I'd be worried, too."

Something twists through me. Something sparks. My pulse

spikes and my hands tighten together like I could twist my fingers off. I could.

"Susie, it's not like that."

"How is it then?"

He wants to talk. There are so many things I want to ask.

Do you like fucking my mother?

Do you know she fakes it with you?

Do you think I would?

Why do you want to talk to me, Susie?

What's this thing you're trying not to do?

Don't say it's nothing. There's someone else you're trying not to be, right there behind your eyes.

I see it.

Look at me.

Please.

34

LOOK, I HARDLY knew the woman. I mean, I barely remember her now.
Clementine Elizabeth Bough.

I once saw a man on a jet-ski shatter through a wave. That's how thinking about her feels. Careening. Crash. I wondered how different it would be if the wave was a brick wall. How he would look on the other side. Remembering her is a lot like this.

The man who came to visit that night, his name was Lance. Lawrence. Something.

"Your momma's friend Lance is coming by," Momma said. She was smiling at herself in the spare bathroom mirror, her makeup bag opened up in the sink. Bottles and tubes and shiny plastic pencils. It was the bathroom with 'the best light' she said, softening the color of her cheeks and darkening her mouth. She couldn't stop smiling, her hands trembling, smearing mascara on her cheek.

She'd brought the radio in with her, and she was listening to something with acoustic guitars and high voices, a steady beat. Something she hummed to, sang a few words.

"Come be pretty with your momma," she said. Letting me see in the mirror as she put her lipstick on me. I watched my own eyes, delighted. Waiting for my face to transform, but it only half did.

"You're so pretty anyway, you don't need makeup," my mother said. Her face was close to mine, and she was still smiling. She was chewing gum—spearmint taint to her breath. I could see the places where her teeth were yellow.

She turned to look through the laundry basket, stashed in the corner.

"C'mere, little girl," she said. Taking two rolled pairs of ankle socks and sliding them up under my t-shirt, changing the shape of my flat chest. "Now you look just like me."

Lance showed up in jeans and work boots, a jacket he kept zipped, covering the lettering on his t-shirt. He was older than my mother, but still young himself. No grey in his hair, thin lines in his face, some of them deep enough to stay even when he wasn't talking or laughing. Even when his face was still.

"You okay to watch some movies, babe?" my mother asked me, covering me with our blanket, tucking me in at the shoulders and hips so my arms could stick out the sides. Handing me a bowl of popcorn. A pack of chocolate-covered peanuts. Salt and sweet.

She and Lance went into the kitchen.

The radio tinned out more acoustic guitars, more quick-moving beats. My mom and Lance talked with voices loud above the music. They laughed a lot, with long silences stretched between.

I only remember this because I'd never met one of my mother's friends before. I only remember him because she'd never brought a man home until that night.

"I don't wanna lie to you, babe. Your momma has a boyfriend. Don't tell Clem about your momma's boyfriend. Okay?"

Look, I barely remember this now, but that doesn't mean I've got it wrong.

35

THIS IS YOUR *Uncle. This is my Friend.*

That slow, sick wave coming up my insides and sloping down my scalp.

Those other things she's said to me.

Open your legs.

Flash.

"Fuck you, Susie."

I say this out loud, looking at my mother as she lies asleep across from me. Naked and weak on murky-white sheets. Passed out, wasted, drunk, drugged, or just very tired, or sexed-out, or whatever. I don't know and I don't care. Her breath catches in the back of her throat in half-snores. She won't wake up.

I guess this is rage, spitting through my nerves so my hands shake as I look through her jacket. Mock-zips, half-sized pockets. But of course she wouldn't leave them there. I dig the blue bag out from under the bed. She's already split the new pictures into their own envelopes. Three packs of three. It doesn't matter which shots are inside. They're all the same, even when they're not.

Behind me, Susie clears his throat. "I didn't know Polaroid cameras even existed anymore." He laughs, but then he pulls the first full picture out. The laugh sucks back down. Vanishes.

The way he stares at me now, it's not the way I thought he would.

"She wouldn't want you to see those," I say. "Not *you*."

Susie flips through the photographs. Black-backed cards.

His bed.

Broken shorts.

My smile over my shoulder.

Flash.

"You look younger than you are in some of these." His voice hovers like it might break. He clears his throat again. "Like you're a child. But you're not *really* a child . . . not so much anymore. Are you? And children . . . they shouldn't . . . "

My eyes are closing. The one in my forehead, it's opening up.

"Hey, kid," Susie says. "Hey, kid. Stop that, please." There's pain in his voice, a kind of pleading.

I pull my hands back out from under my shirt. My nipples sting from the slide of my hands, the way my thumbnails bite in sharp curves. The pinch of my fingers—something I hate, but the camera likes. Something I hate, but I'm supposed to want.

I don't know why in this moment, but it feels like maybe I need to cry.

"Just stop that," he says, rushing his words. "Don't do that. Don't do stuff like that. Please."

He takes my wrists and closes them together, holding my hands against his chest. It would look romantic in a movie or something, but it's not. He's not holding me like he wants to keep me from moving, like he won't let me go. The way he's looking at me, it's like he's horrified. Like he's shaking so hard inside this is the only way he can control it. His pupils spread into wide black circles. His palms are damp against my hands.

"This is fucked up, baby girl," Susie says. "We need to talk. We need to talk."

***

I'm not supposed to leave like this. On my own without proper clothes, without a bag, without strawberry chewing gum to sweeten my mouth. My hair is thick with sleep-grease and my skin burns where the cold outside air hits my sweat. I'm not going far. It's not that I want to leave. It's that I want to breathe by myself for a second, and not care.

My fingers tremble.

I want to smoke.

I guess I got myself addicted, somehow.

My legs are bare. I didn't put socks on before I pulled on my boots. I'm going to get blisters if I don't slow down. Steady *tap-crush* of my steps on concrete, loose gravel popping under the rubber. The breeze roams up my shirt, my nipples pinch tight, and for a moment I don't know if I've ever been so cold.

I'm halfway down the street when I hear a door slam somewhere behind me, and feet pounding up.

"Stop!" he calls.

I stop.

Susie, cheeks pinked up from his hangover, or maybe from the sudden cold air. His eyes are bloodshot. He looks afraid.

"You got a cigarette?" I say. "I really, really want one. Please."

"Sure, kid." He steps forward like he's scared I might bolt. When he gets close enough, he puts an arm around me. Careful, slow, like he needs me to know where all his fingers are. He spreads them across my shoulder, wide-spaced touch.

"Let's get back and I'll give you a cigarette."

"I don't want my mom to see. She wouldn't . . . She doesn't really want me to smoke."

There's a hitch in his step. "She won't see. I won't let her see."

"Will you ask her to stop, Susie? You like me, don't you?

You like me, I think? Will you tell her to stop, Susie? Please tell her to stop."

I'm walking close enough to him to feel the tremors pushing through him. He wipes his free hand across his eyes, down his mouth. He breathes like it's difficult. He does this over and over again.

"You need to put some more clothes on," he says.

I don't know if he's talking about the pictures of me, or just me. If it matters, I don't know. "Okay."

"Good girl. It's cold outside, huh?"

"Yeah."

His voice is trembling. I'm naked under his hand.

36

"IT'S COLD OUTSIDE."
My mother said this, too. Zipping my jacket. Flipping the collar. Covering my feet. That last night in Carris. The night we left.

She was shaking, but not from the chill. Something shooting through her in liquid pulses, stinging her from the inside.

Momma's scared.

I don't know where I was when this came back, but a voice is asking: *Can she take those off?*

Who asks what? What 'those' are. I don't know. I don't know.

"We have to get out of here, honey."

She was in her sheepskin jacket. Her mouth was very red.

"Where's Clem?" I said.

And she started crying like she didn't care I could see.

When this memory came back to me, I was sitting cross-legged on Susie's bed. My mother was fanning fresh Polaroids and I was imagining her and Susie having sex in the space where I sat. My mother's thighs, the curve of his shoulders when they hunch. The lube my mother secrets up herself leaking past the sheets. She'd use the lube because she doesn't really like him.

DOLL CRIMES

Not like I do. Not like me.

"Clem is really angry with your momma," my mother said. "I don't think she . . . I don't think she wants me here anymore."

When I remembered this, a voice was telling me: *Do that. Do that like this.* I'm so dizzy I barely hold up. I'm happy to lie back. The sheets are cool and white as I slide onto them. There's a pounding in my head. It moves through my whole body. Like I'm sleeping through a fever, rolling through a storm.

This is okay, another voice says. It might be my mother's. I don't know.

"She found out about Lance and it's over, baby. We have to go. We have to go. Clem, she's so mad . . . she took a gun to his work. A fucking gun. We need to leave. We need to go."

I don't recall this exactly, because I remember the fear much more. Screaming without thinking, hearing the way my voice tore up my throat. Grasping this idea in my heart and not my head. In my tiny, shaking hands. Holding onto my mother. Her sheepskin lapels, her falling hair.

"But why?"

In my head I saw Clem in a cowboy hat, two pistols at her sides. I saw her facing this guy called Lance—a man who wasn't real to me. But she didn't have two guns. She only had one. A snub-nosed silver thing she kept in her truck, stashed on the floor beneath the passenger seat. I found it once as we drove into town, and when I pulled it out, she and my mother both screamed, zigzagging to the shoulder in a storm of dust to get it out my hands. Like I couldn't be trusted with the thing. Like I was going to press it to their foreheads, slide it up under my chin.

Of course I wasn't going to do those things. The thought of it came years later, scrubbing through the memory. If I had

181

shot them, myself, by accident or on purpose, none of this would have ever happened. Not a single day deeper in.

"Shhh, baby doll. Shhh."

Big blue duffel bag. Shoes and coats. The camera and the film. An envelope full of cash. An envelope full of Polaroids. Pictures of me in a bikini. Flat chest, beaming smile. Beaming at the thought of *Loki*. The puppy they said I could take home if I did what he said. What she told me. If I was good.

What little girl walks around in swimwear when the weather is so cold? I know it was cold that day. I remember.

Flash.

Take it off, he had said.

And my mother said, *I'm here.*

This was what made me uneasy. The uneasiness in her. She was scared in the way she gets that makes me want Clem. Like the day our car broke down on the backroad in from town. Dust and black smoke that smelled like burning plastic. Like the time we missed the last train back. Empty streets and no way home.

"We have to leave now, baby girl. Quickly. Now. Help me get some of our things, okay?"

I don't know if there were sirens in the distance. Probably not. I hear them anyway. Pulsing lights screaming up behind us. My mother's hands shook, frantic, as she shoved clothes into the bag. Hairbrush. Toothbrush. Heels.

"Hurry."

I couldn't have heard any sirens coming. Not through all the ringing in my head. Deafening. Like a gun had just gone off, right beside my ear.

37

SUSIE DRIVES ME to the strip mall twenty minutes out of town. I sit easy in the passenger seat of his old Camry, my hands folded between my knees. The day is rising bright and blue.

I would be afraid, except I'm with him.

I should be afraid, but I'm not.

The strip mall peels into view ahead. A long, flat building with sunshine sparkling white on its roof.

"Go see a movie or something," Susie says. "I'll meet you out front at five. To fetch you, I mean. And bring you . . . home."

The last time I went to the movies, Momma and me sat in the back row. It was the middle of the day, but it was dark in there. Giant people loomed on the screen in wide-angle views and close-up shots. When they spoke, their voices came from all sides. The Uncle who sat next to me told me what to do. I heard his voice just fine, even across all the noise. I fell asleep right after. Mom didn't wake me until the end.

I don't remember what the movie was about.

"You mean *alone?*" I say.

Not even my mother ever asked me to do something like this.

"Watch a . . . " He stops. *"Jesus Christ."* That look again.

An angry man trying not to cry. That crazy mix of vicious energy fighting not to feel too deep. "Watch a cartoon, animation. Disney or something. A kid thing. Please."

"But I'm not a *kid*," I say. I say it because I don't know what he wants me to be. He has this look in his face, like a need. Only I can't read it so well on him.

"You should've been," Susie says.

If he's sad about something, I don't know why.

"Can I get some food, too?"

"Whatever you want."

He keeps one hand on the steering wheel as he digs through his back pocket with the other, lifting himself higher up in his seat. He pulls out his wallet. "Here."

He has a lot of notes in there. He can't want me to take it all.

"No," he says before I can speak. "No, I don't want something from you. Not like that."

"But I didn't try to do anything."

"It's what you thought *I* wanted to try and do."

I think of Yoda. "Do or do not. There is no *try*."

Susie doesn't smile. So much for all his *Star Wars* jokes.

"I'm going to pretend I didn't hear that," he says instead.

Suddenly I don't like him so much.

He cuts through the parking lot and stops at the entrance. It's so early, it's almost empty. There can't be much open yet. There's a word people use to describe a place when it's like this. *Dead*. Even the clerks and assistants busy unbolting doors and switching on lights. Sliding into uniforms, putting on caps.

Dust storms. Automatons.

No pulse, no thoughts. Taking cues. Repeating lines.

Could Susie be real underneath?

I'm calm, but my third eye is opening. I feel fine, but it flutters blood.

"Be back here at five."

"Fuck you."

"No, girl. *Five.*"

When he drives off, I watch him go, but he doesn't wave goodbye.

38

NONE OF THIS happened in any way I really know. I see it anyway. I don't know how much of it is crazy kid-nonsense, tossed together like a junk pile of barbed wire and blunt razor blades. I feel it anyway. The rust, the scratch. The facts.

Uncle Steve waited down at the gate in his car. The drive was long, and mostly through darkness. Backstreet twists and dirt-track roads. I rode up front in my mother's lap, her arms wrapped so tight around me I didn't need my winter jacket, not with her and the heater, and the glowing buzz of Uncle Steve's voice.

"You'll be all right," I heard him say. Over and over again. Talking to my mother, and not to me. "You'll be fine. You'll do great."

The cellphone he gave her was a Nokia, small and black. They don't make those anymore.

"There are people in this world who dream every damn minute of meeting a girl like you. Girls like the two of you."

"I don't know if we can make it alone."

"You'd rather stay and get pushed around by a dyke? By a guy like *Lance?*"

Look, I didn't understand this then. I'm not so sure I understand it even now, but when I asked why Clem wasn't coming with us, my mom started crying again.

Little kids can be shitty. I know.

39

I DRINK COFFEE until it makes my heart beat too fast. The refills are free and the waitress doesn't talk to me like I'm a kid. This is why I stay, I guess. The way it feels like I'm okay to be here. The way it feels safe. The seats around me fill up with singles and duos. Laptops and notebooks. Actual books, too. I don't have anything to occupy my hands or my eyes except the cup in front of me. I test out white sugar versus brown sugar. Sweetener. Sweetener and white sugar. Sweetener and brown. Cup by cup. I don't look at the people around me. Something about them seems too real. The things they're frowning at, mouthing at, even as they sit alone and type stuff or write stuff or make their notes on printed pages. Like the thoughts they're having might really be real.

I only leave the coffee shop when my bladder fills up, my belly pressing too tight against my button-up jeans. I pay. I stand. Probably the coffee shop has its own restroom, but I'm not going to ask.

Something about asking makes me feel afraid. Bathroom stalls, knocks. Hands reaching through the gaps, into them. Doing things that are going to hurt.

Walking out, I see the man who's been staring at me all this time. A gaze I didn't even feel, cutting across to me from a table by the wall. Fat guy, losing hair, hunched behind his laptop. Angled so he can see straight over. Straight at me. He has a murky look in his eyes—the way he watches me move.

I peel the skin off his scalp and watch the blood run into his eyes. Scarlet stripes. He doesn't know why he's blinking so hard as I pass. I catch myself smiling.

What would Susie do? Punch him? Glare at him? Offer me to him?

I don't know. I don't know.

I don't know what I'm supposed to be doing here. In this place. On my own.

Once I've found the bathrooms, I look for the cinemas. I buy a ticket—the first time I've bought my own movie ticket. It's a movie about birds or something. Animals that talk. Drawn animals, not real. Anthropomorphic smiles. I take a seat in the back row, and when the movie starts, I slide off my seat and find a safe space down there in the dark, sheltered between the rows. Lights flicker over my head. Voices boom in surround-sound. It's like falling asleep at the back of a bar, chaos above and around. Laughter, shouting. Screams. Me safe in the darkness. Hidden, tucked away. Too deep down to reach.

***

It's almost seven in the evening when Susie rolls up. I throw the rest of my lime milkshake in the trash as I stand. He rolls down the window. He pops the door.

"You kept me waiting."

"I had to."

The car smells sharp and strange. Bleach-clean, lemon-scented.

"I just had her washed," he says. "That's why I'm a bit late."

Her. At least he loves his car.

I don't know what's happened, but he's breathing too fast, too tight. I don't know why, but his forehead shines.

"Susie, what's happened?"

He shakes his head.

Maybe he wants me all to himself. Maybe he wants me gone, so he'll have my mother all to himself. Maybe he wants us both gone, but needed something from my mother first.

He doesn't put his hand on my leg as we make the short trip down the highway back into town. He doesn't, but I want him to. We pass a roadside billboard, reds faded orange and blues faded green. I couldn't read it if I tried.

We pass the exit that would take us into town, and when I realize we're not slowing, not turning, ice slices me up through the guts. I sit up straight, turn my head to see what's behind us. To see what we're passing.

"Where are we going?"

"Do you trust me?"

"I don't know."

***

We drive into a kind of factory yard. Rubble yard. Metal and broken cars and dust stained black with oil. It's a sharp kind of place, and it smells like blood. Why did he bring me here? To touch me? To fuck me? To be in a place with me where nobody will see? The evening is too warm for this.

We sit in the car with the doors open. Crickets hiss in the bushes beyond the chain-link fence. Hard-skinned things that scream from secret places.

"What are we doing here?" I say.

"Open the glove compartment."

I do, and piles of cash looped in rubber bands tumble out onto my knees. The dirt-metal smell of stained paper. Rolls and rolls of it, smacking to the floor.

"Jesus. This is a lot of money, Susie. Is it yours?"

"No," he says. "It's yours."

It's hard to breathe.

"My mom and me . . . we could buy our house with this. It's enough for that, right? It must be. It looks it. But . . . this isn't my money, Susie. I don't have money like this. My mom and me . . . we struggle every damn day. Her and me, we—"

Susie shifts, turns with his elbow resting up on the back of my seat. His eyes are bright, serious. A glitter in there like he's all high energy, even though his voice is calm. "Your mother has been keeping all the money she's made off you. She's been hiding it from you. This is *your* goddamn money, not hers."

It's hard to talk. My stomach twists. I slide away from him and stumble out the car, on my knees in the open air that smells like rust and iron and tears. Blood. It smells like blood. I want to throw up.

Susie gets out the car, thudding round the side to me. He sits with me in the dirt. Down in the filth and the darkness, his hands on my shoulders.

"You need to listen to me. Your mother is not your friend. Your mother has been making money off you and keeping it for herself. Do you understand this? Do you?" Then, "Don't cry."

"I'm not."

But I am.

"My momma, she—"

"She doesn't love you. You need to accept this right now, little girl. Maybe you'll understand better as time goes on, I don't know. She doesn't love you. It takes a special kind of evil to do . . . this kind of thing to a child. The shit she's been doing to you for . . . how long?"

"Since we left Carris."

He stares at me, wanting me to say more. To answer his question, I guess.

"Since I was . . . I think five. Maybe six."

"She's made you a fucking sex toy. All so she can keep the money for herself."

I wanted to buy an island. A secret island far from the shore. I wanted an island with my own house on it, and a rowboat for my mother to cross the water toward me. I wanted a rope swing hung from an oak tree. I wanted a silver crown. A purple dress. I told her what I wanted, and she laughed. I don't know now why she laughed.

"Where is she?"

Susie sighs. "She's here," he says. "Come on."

He stands and pulls me to my feet. I'm shaking all the way through my knees, and he puts an arm around my waist. Something about the way he does this makes me feel safe. Like he's the oak tree and I'm the branch. We're swaying in the wind.

We walk towards an old storeroom, or maybe it's a warehouse. The sun is going down behind it and it's hard to make out. Black windows too dusty to shine. It's smaller than our house in Carris was. It's bigger than Uncle Steve's.

The door slides open in a rusted metal rush. Susie gropes along the inside of the wall and hits a switch. There's a sick, animal smell in the place.

I turn and press my mouth into Susie's neck. He stiffens, gripping my forearms to push me back. I want to taste the salt on his skin. I want to hear him breathing in my ear, heavy and deep like it matters. The touch that is so total. I guess I want it because I'm scared.

"Stop," he says. "This isn't how you look for comfort."

"But I like you, Susie."

"I know you do. I like you, too. But the day we do anything like that with each other, it won't be like this. I know you don't understand these things yet, but trust me when I tell you this isn't the place and it's not the time."

"Where's my mom?"

"I need you to be strong," Susie says.

We walk to the back of the room.

It's not what I see, it's what I sense. A stillness, too thick to call calm. Like the dust is too fine on the ground, the way it is once it's settled from a storm. Everything in here is cold and sharp. My eyes snap open, all three.

"Susie, what happened?"

For a moment she looks like a twist of dirty blankets, rumpled up on the metal table, obscure in the dark. I take another step and, for a second there, she doesn't look real. Arms thrown back, legs crossed shut below the hips.

Flash.

The space between her legs is dark and stubbled, a sliver of pink flesh peeking through the slit. *Coral Pink*, pretty and wet. Her nipples slide on her chest as she breathes. Her breasts didn't always look like this. So low and so wide, like raw eggs running flat through a hot pan as they hit. What did she tell me?

Don't ever breastfeed.

Her eyes are swollen shut so her face is hardly hers.

I want to brush my teeth.

Susie steps soft toward her, then crouches at her side. He doesn't know it, but there's a scimitar behind his head. It's curved in a half-circle, too black to catch the light. So sharp it shreds the air as it trembles. It hovers against his neck where his blood is closest to the surface. How dark will it be when it slips out his wounds? Staining slide.

My mother moans, her mouth twitching tight over her teeth. She's not wearing lipstick, and with her puffed up eyes this makes her look even stranger—like something not human, like something not her. I step closer on stiff legs. It's then I see the twine around her wrists. The way her hands are wax-blue and white above her head. The red that burns against the cords in raw circles.

I want a four-poster bed, I once said.

"Mom?"

She moans louder, her lips split apart and something the same color and consistency of cappuccino cream slides out her mouth. Frothy white. Her face is turned, or she would choke. It spills into her hair, gold to dark blonde.

"Mom."

Susie stands and spins round to grab me. One arm presses around the back of my head, catching me in a hook. The other closes across my back.

"Momma!"

"You're safe, kid. You're safe with me. Look into my eyes. Here."

But I can't.

Maybe my mother's really fine, and it's my third eye showing me this.

This isn't really happening.

There's no way this is real.

"What did you do to her?"

"I'm holding her down. I'm just keeping her down."

"You fucked her. I know you did."

"That was before."

"Before *what*?"

I should be screaming, but my brain is blurring over. If Susie wasn't holding me my legs would bend.

40

SHE USED TO call me *Angel-Kid*. She used to call me *Doll*.

Look, I hardly knew the woman. At least, that's what my mother said, but I think she tried to help me once. I think she tried to stop this thing.

"Little girls don't need more than two eyes."

I know she never said this. Still, it's her voice that speaks.

41

WHEN SUSIE HOLDS me in this place, he's the one who kisses me. His hands in my hair, his lips on my forehead.

If a man kisses you on the forehead, my mother once said, *it's different to a kiss on the mouth. If he kisses you on the forehead, he feels something more than just sex. Maybe something personal, something just for you.*

"If I weren't the type of guy I am," Susie says, "I'd say we need the police, but the police aren't our friends. They'd throw me away the second they laid eyes on me, it wouldn't matter to them what I have to tell."

"But you're not so bad," I tell him.

"You don't know all I am. Look at what I did to your mother." Then, "Piece of shit." Then, "Cunt."

The way he's angry for me, it feels like I'm supposed to be angry too, but I'm not. She's like a wax figurine with its heart grown wrong. My third eye opens, and I see my shadow falling over her. My hands brush her face, a soft motherly touch. I run my hands down her body, and wherever I touch her, the skin opens up. It peels off, slides back, in a thick sheath as false as rubber. Underneath, red ants swarm. Where her heart used to be, I see a well. Weeds grow up around it, and when I peer into the mouth I see a doll drifting down there. Tiny hands float helplessly in black water.

Sam.

She's too far down to reach.

"We'll leave," Susie says. "We'll leave right now. We'll leave her like this. Maybe she'll wake up, maybe she won't. Maybe someone will find her. Maybe not. We don't care about that, okay, baby doll? We're leaving. We'll leave."

My mother's hand twitches. A spasm in her thumb. Is she calling me? I don't know.

I'm the stillest of rivers.

"Give me a cigarette," I say. I don't think my voice has ever been so calm. Smooth and strong like my mother's. Sure, like I've always wanted to be.

Susie reaches into his jacket pocket and lights me a smoke. He hands it to me and I hold it between my fingers, staring at its glowing tip.

My third eye, it isn't open. I'm seeing this, and it's real.

My mother's warped face is covered in shadows, lined with blood. Blood in all the wrinkles she tries so hard to hide. I'd feel sorry for her if she looked more like herself. I am sorry for her, because I realize now how she can't see.

I cup her face with my left hand. Her skin is wet and cold. I hold the cigarette between my lips, dragging on it so it flares bright as a small, red cherry.

"Open your eyes," I say to my mother.

But she doesn't, because she can't.

I hold the cigarette to her forehead, pressing it into the place where her own third eye needs to be. If she ever had one. If she's even real.

I'm crying but I shouldn't be. Like my body isn't mine.

The tip of the cigarette sears into her skin, burning a circle into her flesh. Let that be her iris. Let that be her only eye.

Behind me, Susie draws in breath between his teeth, a shock-hiss sound of surprise.

I drop the cigarette. I step away.

"Let's go," Susie says.

I want to go.

Home.

EPILOGUE

SUSIE AND ME, we've decided my real age is seventeen. No more plastic bead bracelets, no more pigtails. No more cherry-scented lip gloss or strawberry-flavored gum. My real age is seventeen, we've said, but if anyone asks we tell them I'm eighteen.

It was like a scene from the movie, the way we drove out of town. I sat in the passenger seat with the window rolled down, and it wasn't so cold that I needed any arms around me. I wasn't shivering so bad I couldn't breathe. Maybe it was better than a movie, because usually in real life nobody cares that much. All those close-ups on faces. Panic or tears in the eyes. The parents rushing to the child. The kids rallying around their friend. All those understanding expressions, those touching words and heroic promises. In a movie, the star gets to be everybody's priority. But nobody makes another person more important than them. Nobody puts everything of theirs on hold like that, not for anyone. Except Susie. He cares. Which makes sense, since only beautiful people do beautiful things.

My mother showed me this. I think it's true.

We moved to a city where Susie says the music scene is good.

You ever seen a band play live? he asks me.

DOLL CRIMES

You can wear what you want, he tells me. *You don't have to ask me again.*

When we moved into our apartment, he got me a puppy. I named him Loki. His fur is dust grey and his skin wrinkles up in folds, like a little old man in a baby canine body.

I got my puppy after all.

The money my momma kept from me, it was a lot, but it wasn't as much as I thought. Once we'd signed our lease and bought our furniture, more than half of it was gone already. You need money for new beginnings. I guess my mother didn't know that so well when she first took me away with her. I bought us Persian rugs and a flat-screen TV, and an antique lamp made of marble. It's carved into the shape of an angel, but it doesn't sing me to sleep. It doesn't have to. I have Susie.

Susie's selling drugs again to keep the money coming in, to support him and me in this new life of ours. It helps that he has so many friends. Friends everywhere, all day long, in and out of our home. They guess my age at eighteen, nineteen, but that's because I'm wearing dark lipstick now. I'm dressing how I want. I told Susie I'll never wear heels, and I'm not touching lip gloss ever again.

"Not even if our pals like it?" he asks. Then apologizes. "This won't be like that," he promises me. "You won't ever have to do a single thing you're not okay with. Not ever again."

So no, I don't wear heels when I lie back on his bed for him. For his friends. There is no *Flash*. I keep my eyes shut.

Loki yaps at the door and money changes hands. I get to keep half of it this time. Half of this. It's mine. He doesn't hide it from me. Not a single cent. Half, you know. It's only fair.

"I love you, baby doll," he says. When he holds me close, he says these things. I wake up smiling, tight in his arms. Happy with all the wet between my legs.

"I love you, Susie."

I know exactly where I was when we had this conversation.

I think, this time, maybe I remember everything.

ABOUT THE AUTHOR

Karen Runge is an author and visual artist based in South Africa. She is the author of *Seven Sins: Stories* from Concord Free Press, *Seeing Double* from Grey Matter Press, and *Doll Crimes* from Crystal Lake Publishing. Never shy of darker themes in horror fiction, she has been dubbed 'The Queen of Extreme' and 'Princess of Pain' by various bloggers and book reviewers. Jack Ketchum once said in response to one of her stories: "Karen, you scare me."

THE END?

Not quite . . .

Dive into more Tales from the Darkest Depths:

Novels:

The Mourner's Cradle: A Widow's Journey by Tommy B. Smith
House of Sighs (with sequel novella) by Aaron Dries
The Third Twin: A Dark Psychological Thriller
by Darren Speegle
Aletheia: A Supernatural Thriller by J.S. Breukelaar
Where the Dead Go to Die by Mark Allan Gunnells
and Aaron Dries
Blackwater Val by William Gorman
Pretty Little Dead Girls: A Novel of Murder and Whimsy
by Mercedes M. Yardley
Nameless: The Darkness Comes by Mercedes M. Yardley

Novellas:

Every Foul Spirit by William Gorman
The Pale White by Chad Lutzke
A Season in Hell by Kenneth W. Cain
Quiet Places: A Novella of Cosmic Folk Horror by Jasper Bark
The Final Reconciliation by Todd Keisling
Apocalyptic Montessa and Nuclear Lulu: A Tale of Atomic Love
by Mercedes M. Yardley
Wind Chill by Patrick Rutigliano
Little Dead Red by Mercedes M. Yardley

Anthologies:

Shallow Waters Vol.3: A Flash Fiction Anthology edited by
Joe Mynhardt
Tales from The Lake Vol.5, edited by Kenneth W. Cain
Fantastic Tales of Terror: History's Darkest Secrets,
edited by Eugene Johnson
Welcome to The Show, edited by Doug Murano
and Matt Hayward
Lost Highways: Dark Fictions From the Road,
edited by D. Alexander Ward
Behold! Oddities, Curiosities and Undefinable Wonders, edited by
Doug Murano
Gutted: Beautiful Horror Stories, edited by Doug Murano and
D. Alexander Ward

Short story collections:

Book Haven and Other Curiosities by Mark Allan Gunnells
Darker Days by Kenneth W. Cain
Dead Reckoning and Other Stories by Dino Parenti
Things You Need by Kevin Lucia
Frozen Shadows and Other Chilling Stories by Gene O'Neill
Varying Distances by Darren Speegle
The Ghost Club: Newly Found Tales of Victorian Terror by
William Meikle
Ugly Little Things: Collected Horrors by Todd Keisling
Whispered Echoes by Paul F. Olson
Embers: A Collection of Dark Fiction by Kenneth W. Cain

Poetry collections:

The Place of Broken Things by Linda D. Addison and
Alessandro Manzetti
WAR by Alessandro Manzetti and Marge Simon
Brief Encounters with My Third Eye by Bruce Boston
No Mercy: Dark Poems by Alessandro Manzetti
Eden Underground: Poetry of Darkness by Alessandro Manzetti

If you've ever thought of becoming an author, we'd also like to recommend these non-fiction titles:

It's Alive: Bringing Your Nightmares to Life, edited by Eugene Johnson and Joe Mynhardt

The Dead Stage: The Journey from Page to Stage by Dan Weatherer

Where Nightmares Come From: The Art of Storytelling in the Horror Genre, edited by Joe Mynhardt and Eugene Johnson

Horror 101: The Way Forward, edited by Joe Mynhardt and Emma Audsley

Horror 201: The Silver Scream Vol.1 and *Vol.2*, edited by Joe Mynhardt and Emma Audsley

Modern Mythmakers: 35 interviews with Horror and Science Fiction Writers and Filmmakers by Michael McCarty

Writers On Writing: An Author's Guide Volumes 1,2,3, and 4, edited by Joe Mynhardt. Now also available in a Kindle and paperback omnibus.

Or check out other Crystal Lake Publishing books for more Tales from the Darkest Depths.

Hi readers,

It makes our day to know you reached the end of our book. Thank you so much. This is why we do what we do every single day.

Whether you found the book good or great, we'd love to hear what you thought. Please take a moment to leave a review on Amazon, Goodreads, or anywhere else readers visit. Reviews go a long way to helping a book sell, and will help us to continue publishing quality books. You can also share a photo of yourself holding this book with the hashtag #IGotMyCLPBook!

Thank you again for taking the time to journey with Crystal Lake Publishing.

We are also on . . .

Website:
www.crystallakepub.com

Be sure to sign up for our newsletter and receive three eBooks for free: http://eepurl.com/xfuKP

Books:
http://www.crystallakepub.com/book-table/

Twitter:
https://twitter.com/crystallakepub

Facebook:
https://www.facebook.com/Crystallakepublishing/

Instagram:
https://www.instagram.com/crystal_lake_publishing/

Patreon:
https://www.patreon.com/CLP

Or check out other Crystal Lake Publishing books for more Tales from the Darkest Depths. You can also subscribe to Crystal Lake Classics (http://eepurl.com/dn-1Q9), where you'll receive fortnightly info on all our books, starting all the way back at the beginning, with personal notes on every release. Or follow us on Patreon (https://www.patreon.com/CLP) for behind the scenes access, bonus short stories, polls, interviews, and if you're interested, author support.

With unmatched success since 2012, Crystal Lake Publishing has quickly become one of the world's leading indie publishers of Mystery, Thriller, and Suspense books with a Dark Fiction edge.

Crystal Lake Publishing puts integrity, honor, and respect at the forefront of our operations.

We strive for each book and outreach program that's launched to not only entertain and touch or comment on issues that affect our readers, but also to strengthen and support the Dark Fiction field and its authors.

Not only do we publish authors who are legends in the field and as hardworking as us, but we look for men and women who care about their readers and fellow human beings. We only publish the very best Dark Fiction, and look forward to launching many new careers.

We strive to know each and every one of our readers while building personal relationships with our authors, reviewers, bloggers, podcasters, bookstores, and libraries.

Crystal Lake Publishing is and will always be a beacon of what passion and dedication, combined with overwhelming teamwork and respect, can accomplish: unique fiction you can't find anywhere else.

We do not just publish books, we present you worlds within your world, doors within your mind from talented authors who sacrifice so much for a moment of your time.

This is what we believe in. What we stand for. This will be our legacy.

Welcome to Crystal Lake Publishing.

THANK YOU FOR PURCHASING THIS BOOK!

Printed in Great Britain
by Amazon